DR. DOLITTLE. AS A CONFIRMED ANIMAL LOVer, this has always been one of my favorite stories. As a child, I thought that being able to talk to the animals would be wonderful indeed. And as an adult, I have to admit it would certainly be convenient.

When my dog wants me to take her out at two A.M., it would be great to be able to tell her to wake up my husband instead and know she'd do it. And when my cat sits in the middle of the floor and yowls for no apparent reason, it would be terrific to be able to ask her to stop and know that she would. And when my sons' goldfish make a suicide pact with each other and begin floating belly-up one by one, it would be helpful to talk to the survivors and ask them what went wrong. If I could talk to the animals, I would be lucky indeed.

But suppose, just suppose, the lucky individual who could chat with animals was an absolutely gorgeous veterinarian with broad shoulders and golden-brown eyes? And suppose he doesn't believe it because he doesn't believe in the unexplainable? And what would happen if this gorgeous man who doesn't believe in magic meets an enchanting sprite of a woman who believes in it with all her heart?

I believe in magic—the magic that happens when a man and woman fall in love. And nothing could be more delightful than to share a little of this magic with you.

Bonnie Pega

WHAT ARE *LOVESWEPT* ROMANCES?

They are stories of true romance and touching emotion. We believe those two very important ingredients are constants in our highly sensual and very believable stories in the LOVESWEPT *line. Our goal is to give you, the reader, stories of consistently high quality that may sometimes make you laugh, sometimes make you cry, but are always fresh and creative and contain many delightful surprises within their pages.*

Most romance fans read an enormous number of books. Those they truly love, they keep. Others may be traded with friends and soon forgotten. We hope that each LOVESWEPT *romance will be a treasure—a "keeper." We will always try to publish*

LOVE STORIES YOU'LL NEVER FORGET
BY AUTHORS YOU'LL ALWAYS REMEMBER

The Editors

ANIMAL MAGNETISM

BONNIE
PEGA

BANTAM BOOKS
NEW YORK • TORONTO • LONDON • SYDNEY • AUCKLAND

ANIMAL MAGNETISM
A Bantam Book / January 1994

If you would be interested in receiving protective vinyl covers for your Loveswept books, please write to this address for information:

Loveswept
Bantam Books
P.O. Box 985
Hicksville, NY 11802

ISBN 0-553-44406-9

Published simultaneously in the United States and Canada

Bantam Books are published by Bantam Books, a division of Bantam Doubleday Dell Publishing Group, Inc. Its trademark, consisting of the words "Bantam Books" and the portrayal of a rooster, is Registered in U.S. Patent and Trademark Office and in other countries. Marca Registrada. Bantam Books, 1540 Broadway, New York, New York 10036.

PRINTED IN THE UNITED STATES OF AMERICA

OPM 0 9 8 7 6 5 4 3 2 1

ONE

Sebastian Kent looked up from the box of veterinary supplies he was unpacking and eyed the female standing in the doorway. Her small size and sweet face made her seem barely old enough to cross the street without permission. Her body, however, had the lush curves that could only belong to a grown woman. Sebastian's appreciative gaze ran over those curves before he looked up to meet her eyes. He smiled politely. "May I help you?"

"You're the new vet, aren't you? I'm Danni Sullivan." She walked in, reached out, and gave him a surprisingly firm handshake, then perched on the edge of an unpacked carton.

Danni? No, she didn't look at all like a Danni. That name suggested a jeans-clad, sneaker-shod tomboy with her hair in a no-nonsense braid.

This girl looked more like an Esmerelda or a Priscilla. Golden-blond hair cascaded around her shoulders, and the violet-blue satin band holding it back was the same color as her eyes. Her features were dainty, and she couldn't have been more than five feet tall.

She wore a gathered purple gauze skirt paired with a snug pink sweater and pink lace tights. Tiny pink fairies swung from her ears, and her shoes were impossibly tiny ballet slippers. All in all, she looked like a butterfly—a pink-and-purple butterfly.

"Well, Miss—er—Ms. Sullivan, I'm Dr. Kent. Sebastian Kent. Is there something I can do for you?" He suddenly realized he was staring at the pink sweater stretching over her pert breasts. *Get a grip, man, she's just a kid.* With an effort, he relocated his gaze upward. Nice lips. Soft and just a little pouty. Damn. He'd obviously been celibate too long.

"I'd like to apply for a job."

"A job?" Sebastian echoed stupidly. "Won't it interfere with, uh, your schoolwork?"

"Oh, no. I only take classes three days a week." Danni smiled.

"They have high school only three days a week?"

Danni's smile widened. "I'm in college."

3

Sebastian revised his estimate of her age from sixteen to eighteen.

She continued. "I drive into Norfolk on Monday, Tuesday, and Thursday. It's a good forty minutes, but I don't mind it. I really like to drive. I use the time to think. I drove all the way from Florida to Bar Harbor, Maine, summer before last. That was a great drive. Have you ever seen the coast of Maine?"

That was obviously a rhetorical question because she went on without giving him a chance to respond. "It's beautiful. I've never seen a rocky coastline before. It wasn't at all like the coast along the Gulf that I saw when I drove to New Orleans last summer. Now that's some city. I was totally amazed by New Orleans. It's so alive, so full of history. I found Lewis there, in a little shop on Bourbon Street, and brought him home. Anyway, I don't mind the drive into Norfolk. It's worth it. I'm working on my second degree."

"Second-degree what?" Sebastian shook his head as if to clear it. He wasn't making heads or tails out of this conversation. And who the hell was Lewis?

"I already have one degree," Danni explained patiently. "In art education. Only I decided I didn't want to teach. Might have a discipline problem with the students towering over me.

So I decided to go back and get another degree."

Sebastian revised her age up another three or four years and felt relieved that she was a lot older than she looked.

Danni absently twirled a strand of hair around her finger and went on, "I started out in business, but the subject didn't interest me very much, so I transferred to English Lit. Great subject to study, but, as I said, I don't want to teach. I'd almost decided on medicine—anesthesiology or nursing—but I hate hospitals and such. So I decided on veterinary medicine. I've always loved animals, and I get along really well with them."

"I see," Sebastian murmured. He didn't, but she seemed to be waiting for a response.

"Anyway, I think I should work here with you on Wednesdays, Fridays, and Saturdays while school is in session. I graduate in six weeks, then I'll be able to help you every day—well, until midsummer. Then I plan on looking around for a job in a clinic someplace exciting, so you'll probably want to hire someone else.

"You are going to have Saturday hours, aren't you? I think most of the folks here expect you to. Dr. Adams took off Sundays and Tuesdays. You can take off any days you want, of course, but I think you should definitely have Saturday hours."

"Uh, yes, I had planned on Saturday hours."

"Great!" Danni exclaimed. "It will work out perfectly, then."

"What will work out?" Lord, but he was confused.

"My working for you."

"Working for me? Doing what?"

"Why, your paperwork, of course. Or anything else that needs doing."

"Of course," Sebastian murmured, feeling as if he'd been hit on the head. With a pink-and-purple feather.

"I can help out with minor injuries too. I've been doing that since Dr. Adams left last spring. I hated for the local folks to drive to the vet over in Greenston for things like minor cuts or mange or flea baths. I wouldn't mind doing that kind of thing again. You can do Peanut, though."

"Peanut?"

"Mrs. Walling's pet bull."

"Pit bull?"

"No, pet bull. Brahma. Her son originally got him as a Four-H project, but Mrs. Walling became attached to him. He's prone to skin problems in the summer heat and has to be bathed and conditioned every week. He hates water, though, and puts up quite a fuss. He runs when he sees me coming these days because I'm the only one who can manage his bath. I'll give you some pointers on handling him, if you like. He's really just a big baby."

Sebastian couldn't help smiling at the image of this petite blonde wrestling with a bull. A brahma, no less. Yet, somehow, it didn't surprise him at all that she *could* manage it. He had the feeling that if Danni Sullivan wanted something badly enough, she wouldn't let a little thing like several thousand pounds of weight stop her. "Some pointers would be nice, Ms. Sullivan. Look, I—"

"Please call me Danni."

"Danni. Well, Danni, I'm not sure I'll have enough work to keep you busy."

"You'll be busier than you think. The folks around here are going to take a real shine to you—not to mention their animals."

Sebastian stifled a sigh. He didn't want to come right out and say that she was not at all the sort of person he pictured as his receptionist. In New York his receptionist had been a middle-aged woman who'd taken her job as seriously as if she'd been receptionist to a world-famous surgeon. Danni Sullivan looked too flighty to give something as mundane as office work the attention it needed.

Something happened as he looked at her, preparing to say no. He'd have sworn her eyes twinkled at him. He'd heard that expression, but in all his thirty-four years had never seen it happen. But, he was sure, Danni Sullivan's violet eyes twinkled, flashing little gold sparks. Sparks of humor, mischief, whimsy. Life.

He wasn't exactly sure why, but he found himself smiling back. Stranger still, he found himself hiring the mercurial Miss Sullivan. It was probably a huge mistake. There was no telling what her filing system would be like. Besides, not only did she talk circles around him, but she was entirely too appealing. That could only get in the way.

And she confused him. Intrigued him. Made him smile. It had been a long, long time since anyone had done that.

"What was he like?" Virgie Pace, Danni's grandmother, asked as soon as Danni walked into the newly renovated farmhouse the two shared.

Danni tossed her purse into the overstuffed chair by the front door and perched on the arm. "He seemed very nice, Gran. A little stuffy, though, especially for White Creek. Dress shoes, sharp pleats in his trousers." But those trousers did fit great buns, she thought. And the white shirt he'd worn covered broad shoulders and powerful arms. She didn't say it out loud, however. Her grandmother would have started knitting baby booties.

Virgie had often said she wanted nothing more than to see her granddaughter married and settled. Danni didn't want either. There was a wide, wonderful world out there, and she intended to see and do a whole lot more before she got married. If she ever did.

"Did you get the job?"

"Mm-hm. I start . . . well, we actually didn't set a date. I guess I should go over there after class tomorrow to help him get things organized."

"Organized? You?" Virgie looked up, a wide grin splitting her pleasantly wrinkled face. "Since when, Danielle?"

"I can organize things that matter," Danni said in amused self-defense. "It's just that most things we spend time and energy on aren't worth it. Much better to take life as it comes, don't you think? Most people plan things to death."

Her grandmother murmured assent, and Danni went on. "Take Dr. Kent. He was surrounded by boxes, and they weren't only labeled as to the rooms they belong in, but each had a list of its contents. And he had *another* list in his hand—probably a list of his lists. That's too much. He needs to spend more time smelling the coffee or the roses or whatever, and less time making lists."

With those words hanging in the air, Danni went back to the sun room and settled in her favorite overstuffed sofa with her biology book and remarkably well-organized notes.

Several hours later, she lay in her four-poster bed, staring up at the faint design in the lace canopy outlined by the moonlight and thinking about the intriguing Dr. Sebastian Kent. He was very attractive, but she couldn't help thinking how much more attractive he would be if his hair were just an inch or two longer. Those dark brown waves might turn into tousled curls. She sighed. She'd always been a sucker for curly hair on men.

And if he wore jeans instead of tailored khaki trousers, he'd be drop-dead gorgeous. She closed her eyes and let her mind draw the picture—curly hair, snug jeans, maybe a T-shirt. But when she found herself imagining how well those jeans would pull over his firm thighs, she decided it would be best if she tried to go to sleep. She sat up, gave her pillow a determined fluff, and lay back down.

What a shame he couldn't loosen up just a little. She smiled. But then, maybe she could help him. After all, she was the least stuffy person she knew.

Sebastian couldn't keep Danni Sullivan out of his mind. She dressed with the flamboyance of a circus performer and exuded an innocent sensuality that left him feeling tongue-tied—although the way she talked—fast, in dizzying circles, with lightning changes of subject, he doubted he'd get to say much to her anyway. She was, without a doubt, the strangest woman he'd ever met—including all those in New York City.

There'd been the society matron who'd insisted her cat needed a psychiatrist; the corporate executive who'd made her husband sleep in the guest room so her six French poodles could sleep on her bed; and Martha, the owner of the deli across the street from his office, who'd insisted on carrying her cockatoo with her to the fortune-teller she frequented.

But next to Danni Sullivan, they all seemed downright uninteresting. Part of him hoped that she'd forget she'd been hired. The other part of him couldn't wait for her to show up for work. To say she aroused conflicting emotions in him was putting it mildly.

So he wasn't at all surprised when the object of his thoughts suddenly appeared behind him. He didn't know just how he knew those footsteps were hers, but he knew. He turned around and shook his head a little. Yep, she still looked like a butterfly. A very sexy butterfly.

Again she wore pink and purple, but this time the purple skirt and pink lace tights had been replaced by snug-fitting pink stirrup pants and a purple knit top. Her incredible mane of hair was tied with a purple lace ribbon into a ponytail on top of her head. Sebastian didn't know why she had reminded him of a young girl the first time he'd seen her. She was all woman.

Was it the way those stretch pants outlined her shapely thighs? Maybe it was the way the lacy knit top allowed tantalizing glimpses of the creamy flesh beneath. Or was it the hair? The first time he'd seen her, it had hung in a silky sweep—making her look for all the world like Alice in Wonderland. Now, with her hair pulled away from her face, her high cheekbones, patrician nose, and killer eyes were prominent.

Flighty? Probably. Mercurial? Yes. Sexy as hell? Definitely.

"Uh, hi." *Right, old man, grab her attention with your sparkling conversation.*

Danni gave Sebastian a smile that he could only describe as shy, and he felt a strange clutching in his stomach.

"Hi," she said, slinging a well-worn backpack in the corner. "I got out of class early and thought

I'd come by and see what I could help you with. What do you need unpacked?"

"Nothing. I mean, not yet. The place needs a little cleaning."

Danni eyed the debris piled in the corners. "I think old Mr. Marshall might lend you his bulldozer."

"It does look daunting, doesn't it?"

"If it were anyone else, it would take into next week," Danni muttered, and pushed up her sleeves. "But since it's me, we'll have this done by the end of the day. I work fast, and I have superb organizational skills."

"I'm sure you do. And thanks for offering, but I can manage." He didn't mean to sound cool, but he felt it would be better—especially for his sanity—to keep a strictly professional distance between them.

"Nonsense! What are assistants for, anyway? So, where would you like me to get started?"

She had already promoted herself from receptionist to assistant, and she hadn't even started work yet. "You mean receptionist," he corrected her.

She waved her hand. "Whatever. Suppose I take the front room?"

"Danni, you're not dressed to go around cleaning out century-old farmhouses." Actually, he liked the way she was dressed, but unless she changed clothes, he didn't know how much work he'd get done. He'd be too busy watching the pull of the stretch fabric of her trousers over her rounded bottom.

She paused and looked down at herself. "You got me there. Especially since I really get into things—and I attract dirt like a magnet. I'll run home and change. Be back in a flash."

Sebastian bent, picked up a cardboard box he was using to haul trash, then turned back. "It's really not—" She was gone. He'd turned his head for all of a split second. How had she vanished so quickly? She'd have had to go right by him to leave the room, but she hadn't. Had she?

Sebastian wiped his hand over his eyes. Was he seeing things? Or, more accurately, not seeing things? Or could she really vanish like the Cheshire cat in Alice in Wonderland?

He was still mulling this over when Danni was "back in a flash," as she'd said she would be. "You, uh, you certainly made it back quickly," Sebastian said.

"Oh, I live a hop, skip, and a jump from here."

"Hop, skip, and a jump?"

"Sure. I just hopped out the window—" She indicated the open window behind her.

Sebastian sighed in relief.

"Then I skipped down the path in the back, and I jumped across Denning's Creek. Hop, skip, and a jump, you see?"

"I see," he murmured dryly. He saw, all right. He saw that being confused around Danni Sullivan was probably going to be a permanent state of affairs.

He noticed her choice of clothes. Pink and purple. Again. This time snug purple jeans hugged her bottom and her firm breasts were outlined nicely by a pink T-shirt. When Sebastian found his gaze lingering on her breasts, he looked quickly away. He'd never been one to ogle women. He thought it was crude, but something about Danni seemed to invite his stare. He searched for something to say. "Ah, you seem to like purple and pink a great deal."

Danni looked at him wide-eyed. "I'd better. Magda told me they're my colors."

"Magda? Who's Magda?"

"Magda lives at the head of Denning's Creek, right where it bubbles out of the ground—it's from an underground spring, you know. That's why it's icy cold all year. We used to go swimming there when I was a kid. I spent summers at Gran's with my cousin Annabelle, but we never could stay in the water longer than fifteen minutes. Our toes would turn blue.

"Anyway, Magda lives there. She says she's descended from a Gypsy, but Gran swears she's from up in Waverly. Says they went to school together."

"Did Magda take one of those season-color seminars?"

Danni looked mystified as she twirled a curl around her finger. "I don't think so. But they sound intriguing. You'll have to tell me about them. Magda knows what colors are good for people to wear. What colors bring them luck, so to speak."

"And you believe that stuff?"

"Of course. Why shouldn't I?"

Dammit! She did it again. Twinkled those eyes at him. But was she inviting him to laugh along *with* her, or daring him to laugh *at* her? He did the safe thing and simply gave a noncommittal nod.

"You should be meeting Magda shortly. It's about time for her cats to be vaccinated."

"Should I set up an appointment for her to come in?"

"No, you'll need to go out there. She has too many cats to bring in."

"How many does she have?"

"Twenty-six at last count, I think." Danni grinned at the look on his face.

"Twenty-six?"

"Hey, I told you I thought you'd be kept pretty busy here. We're a small town, but just about everyone has an animal or two."

"Or twenty-six?"

"Yep." She grinned again. She knew that she had Sebastian thoroughly confused. She'd often been told she had that effect on people. But she enjoyed seeing tiny little bits of his cool, controlled veneer flake off. She had a real hankering to see what kind of man lay beneath.

There was another reason she liked seeing him slightly off balance, she admitted. When he was trying to keep up with her, the shadows in his eyes disappeared. No one should have shadows like that in his eyes. She wondered what had happened to put them there. And, more important, what she could do to get rid of them.

"Sounds like Magda could use her own personal vet. So is that why Dr. Adams left—too many patients ran him ragged?"

"Possibly, though he held out a good number of years. He retired at eighty-three, you know." Danni gave him an assessing look. "I wonder how long you'll last."

"Are you asking me about my staying power?" Sebastian raised an eyebrow.

Danni stared at him a long moment before it registered that there had been a tinge of suggestiveness to his tone of voice. She'd caught a glimmer of a virile, sensual, dangerous man beneath the staid, professional exterior. Maybe she shouldn't be in such a hurry to chip off that facade after all, she thought. He was sexy enough as it was. If any more sex appeal shone through, she'd be in real trouble.

"Cat got your tongue?" Sebastian smiled and handed her a broom. "Here."

She ran her tongue over her bottom lip, but stopped when she noticed his gaze following the movement. "What's this?"

"And you're working on a second degree? It's a broom. You hold on to the handle and move the bristles back and forth over the floor. It's a primitive cleaning device." His smile widened.

"I know that," she muttered. "I mean, what's this for?"

"Did you, or did you not, volunteer your help?"

"Um, yes. Yes, I did. Where would you like me to start?"

"How about in the front room? Most of the debris is out of there already. All it needs now is a little spit and polish."

"Right. Sure. No problem."

They discussed movies while they worked, hollering comments back and forth—Danni in the front room, Sebastian in the back. They disagreed on almost every movie, but it didn't matter. Their arguments were spirited and amiable. The only problem Danni had with it was that she would have loved to see Sebastian's face while they talked.

Finally, Danni dropped the sponge back into the bucket of water with a splash and wiped the back of her hand across the beads of sweat on her forehead, leaving streaks of dirt. When she'd told Sebastian she "got into" her work, she hadn't been exaggerating.

Unfortunately, she also had a penchant for dirt—or rather, it had a penchant for her. Smudges of dust and dirt adorned her hands and clothes, and cobwebs frosted her ponytail. She peeked into the other room and saw Sebastian cleaning the windows. He'd accomplished a lot in a couple of hours. The room was immaculate. So was he.

Danni looked down at herself and sighed. She knew she looked more like someone who'd just survived a dust storm, while the pleats in his trousers were still perfect. She had an urge to muss his perfection—ruffle his hair, unbutton his shirt an extra button. That wasn't such a good idea, she thought, and pushed it right back out of her head. She was about to duck into the bathroom and rinse her face and hands when Sebastian looked up.

"I'm almost finished in here. How about you?"

"Oh, I'm done too. Except for the windows." From the way he was looking at her, she wondered if her wayward thoughts had telegraphed themselves on her face. His gaze moved over her in slow, lazy appraisal, leaving heat in its wake.

"I'll do those."

He was still looking at her, and Danni began to fidget uncomfortably. She searched for something to say, and her attention fell to the large yellow-striped tomcat that sat in one corner of the room grooming its shaggy fur. "Who's your friend?" She nodded in the cat's direction.

Sebastian shrugged. "I have no idea. He showed up yesterday and followed me around for a while, then showed up again this morning and howled outside the back door until I invited him in for breakfast. He's a strange one, though. He wouldn't touch the can of tuna I opened—people tuna—but went nuts over cornflakes and milk. You don't suppose he belongs to this Magda, do you?"

"I don't know." Danni shook her head. "It's possible, I guess. Her house is a straight shot up the creek. Well, actually, it's around the bend past Willard's pasture, in a spot we call the flats. It's a little marshy in spots. Anyway, he wouldn't have had far to come. Have you noticed he has one green eye and one blue eye?"

"I noticed that last night. Can you call her and find out if he's one of hers?"

"No. She doesn't believe in telephones, says it's too much of a newfangled gadget. Funny, though, she does have a VCR and a CD player. You can ask her if he's hers when you go to vaccinate her cats."

"Oh, right. I ought to go sometime this week, then."

"I could help," Danni suggested hopefully. "It might be useful to have an extra pair of hands when dealing with twenty-six cats."

"I suppose." Sebastian looked down at his hands and grimaced. He needed to wash up. But Danni needed it more, he acknowledged as he looked at her. Strange though, how the smudges on her face emphasized a classic peaches-and-cream complexion.

And there was a smudge on the front of her T-shirt across the curve of her breast. Sebastian's fingers twitched with the desire to reach out and brush away that smudge. He even found himself stretching out a hand and, at the last moment, directed it up to brush aside a cobweb clinging to a stray curl that fell over her forehead.

Danni smiled self-consciously. "I told you I really get into my work. You should see me when I've been gardening. I'm usually covered with water and mud."

"I can imagine," he murmured. The trouble was, he *could* imagine—too well. He had a sudden sharp image of her in a clinging wet T-shirt. He brought his hand up to rub the back of his neck. Thoughts like that were dangerous. After all, he should have learned a lesson by now about getting involved with butterflies. Hadn't one been enough?

Sebastian's features hardened, and he turned away. He began methodically to put away all his cleaning materials. Danni joined in without a word.

"I'll finish in here," Sebastian said politely. "Why don't you go on home? I really appreciate your help, but you missed lunch. I'd hate to see you miss your dinner too."

"Nonsense. I always finish what I start. It should take only a few more minutes to find a cupboard where I can stuff all this. And speaking of missing meals, how are you managing?"

"I have a few odds and ends to make do with until I get a chance to go to the grocery store."

"What are you having for supper tonight?"

"I'll have a can of beef stew or chili."

Danni grimaced. "Gross. I'd invite you to my house for dinner, but Gran and I are eating at Maud Greeley's. It's the monthly meeting of the beautification committee. But tomorrow night, please come to my house. Gran always has enough to feed two or three extra people. I'll ask her to fix Smithfield ham and pineapple casserole."

"I've heard Smithfield ham is a Virginia specialty."

"Haven't you ever had it?"

"Can't say that I have."

"Well then, you're in for a real treat. And you'll love her pineapple casserole too."

"I couldn't impose. I'll spend tomorrow evening looking over some things. I could use the time to catch up on my reading."

"Impose? No such thing. Why, we're neighbors. Come on," she urged. "I'll ask Gran to make some homemade chocolate-chip oatmeal cookies."

"Chocolate chip?"

Danni could have sworn she heard a swiftly hidden trace of wistfulness in his voice. No doubt about it. You could always get to a man by way of his stomach—especially when he'd been eating out of cans for a while. "The best oatmeal cookies this side of the Blue Ridge Mountains. She adds extra chocolate chips and chopped walnuts." She could almost see his mouth watering, but she just smiled and picked up a small carton. "This is the last one. Where shall I put it?"

"Leave it there. Those are mousetraps. I've got enough to put one in each room and two in the kitchen."

"Mousetraps?" Danni didn't especially like small, furry pink-tailed rodents, but the thought of setting traps for them made her cringe.

"I, uh, I don't know if I can. . . ." Her voice trailed off when Sebastian placed a strange-looking contraption in her hand. It was a rectangular box with a funny little door that slid down over the front. "What's this?"

"That's the mousetrap."

"It's not like any I've ever seen."

"It's a cruelty-free mousetrap. You open the sliding door and secure it on top. Then you place the bait in here and set the trigger. The door snaps shut when the mouse takes the bait, so you can let him go. Outside."

Danni's heart turned to pure mush. This six-foot-tall macho-oozing doc even cared about tiny little four-footed critters. Merciful heavens, but he was appealing. And boy, was she in trouble!

TWO

They finished setting up the mousetraps, and Danni glanced at her watch. "Omigosh, I've got to go! I don't want to be late. I'm the chairman. What time do you want me here in the morning?"

Sebastian stared at her blankly. "In the morning?"

"For our first day as the official White Creek Veterinary Clinic. We're all clean, and all we have to do now is finish putting away supplies and such, and we can do that in between patients tomorrow. I don't expect there will be a huge number of patients the first day, do you? I have a great idea for arranging the hospital area. Did I tell you? We should segregate the recuperating animals from the boarders, of course, and we . . ."

She continued talking while Sebastian idly noted her use of the word "we." He wondered if it was the royal "we" or if she was beginning to consider herself a partner, not just an assistant.

"Well, then, I'll be over at nine."

"Uh, sure. See you then. Wait. Isn't tomorrow Tuesday? What about your classes?"

"No problem. I'll get a friend of mine to tape the morning lectures for me, and both my afternoon labs are canceled, anyway. See ya."

With bouncing steps Danni left. Sebastian peeked through the curtain and watched her walk down the street. There was a natural exuberance in her stride that made her hair, glistening in the early evening sun, swing from side to side.

And it made Sebastian begin to catch a faint glimmer of what had been missing in his life the past few years. Enthusiasm. Zest. Lord, she had so much energy. Maybe that's why she talked so fast—she was so full of vitality that she couldn't contain it all, and overflowed in speech.

He felt like a man who was chilled to the bone, reaching out to the warmth of a flame. Was some part of him yearning to recapture the enthusiasm in life he'd lost along the way? Or, rather, had been torn out by the roots? He sighed, dropped the curtain back into place, and turned away.

26

Danni didn't show up until twenty after nine, but then Sebastian hadn't really expected her to be on time. He simply figured she operated on her own time schedule. Butterflies didn't punch time clocks.

"Good morning," she chirped as she pushed the screen door open with her foot. In her left hand she balanced a box that held two ceramic cups of steaming coffee. In her right hand she held an attractive potted plant in a wicker basket.

She set the box on the table. "I didn't know if you drank coffee or not, but I brought a cup just in case. I have one decaf and one regular. I usually drink the decaf because I stay a little wired as it is, but if you'd rather have it, I don't mind drinking the regular."

"I'll take the regular. Thanks." No way did Danni need a boost from caffeine . . . or anything else. He took the cup she indicated and sipped the hot liquid.

Danni took out the other cup. "Where would you like your spathiphyllum?"

"My what?"

"Your spathiphyllum. Peace lily. I brought it to decorate the waiting room. It *is* kind of boring in here, don't you think?"

He hadn't thought about it one way or the other. He looked from side to side, studying the room as if seeing it for the first time. Except for the old-fashioned wallpaper, it was a little bland. At least it had been bland until Danni Sullivan walked in and filled it with color and shimmering energy. "Put the plant anywhere." He waved a vague hand. "Do you think anyone will know we're open today?" He was using "we" too, he noted.

Danni set the plant on the table in the middle of the floor. "I ran by Bosco Wilson's Food Mart this morning and told him."

"And that'll do it?"

"Sebastian, this is a small town. Believe me, that'll do it."

"Telephone, telegraph, and tell a Bosco?"

Danni grinned. "Something like that. Plus Gran's going to the garden-club luncheon today, and she'll tell anyone who hasn't already heard from Bosco."

The word spread well. By lunch they'd had two dogs in for their distemper/rabies boosters, another dog with mange, a kitten with conjunctivitis, even a listless lamb. Danni found herself watching Sebastian as he tended to the various animals. He spoke to the animals, caressed them gently, demonstrating a genuine fondness that the animals responded to. Even Mr. Mueller's cantankerous old hound wagged his tail and made little yipping sounds like a puppy.

She could see why Sebastian had chosen to be a vet. He was a natural. By midafternoon, when things slowed down, she had developed a tremendous respect for him. He was gentle, thorough, eminently competent. She was glad she had the chance to work with him. He was the kind of vet she wanted to be—though not quite so uptight.

While Sebastian waited to see if anyone else was going to come by, he opened the last box of supplies he'd brought and put them away. Danni sat in the corner looking through notes from school.

Sebastian kept sneaking glances at her as he worked. Her head leaned almost pensively against her hand, and the only time she moved at all was when she turned a page. Her very stillness intrigued him. When she talked, she talked fast, her hands fluttering wildly. Like a butterfly, she seemed barely to alight on one flower before flitting to the next. Now, the butterfly rested in the sun, her only movements the occasional wafting of her wings.

He wondered what she was thinking as her forehead wrinkled at something she read. When she gave a small sigh, he asked her.

"Hm?" She looked up.

"You, ah, seemed bothered by something you read."

"It's about, um, you know, putting an animal to sleep. That must be horrible. How do you handle it?"

He leaned against the counter. "The first time I ever had to euthanize an animal, it was a sixteen-year-old poodle named Daisy. She was blind in one eye, partly deaf, had hip dysplasia, and had lost most of her bowel and bladder control. The owner sat with the dog's head in her lap petting Daisy until she closed her eyes. She cried, I cried. When the owner left, I threw up. It was one of the hardest things I've ever had to do."

"But sometimes it's necessary."

"Oh, yes. I think the only way you *can* handle it, is to remind yourself of that. Of course, every once in a while, you get some idiot who wants you to get rid of an animal because it's convenient for him. That's where I draw the line."

"What do you mean?"

"Well, for instance, I knew a man in New York who routinely brought in litters of kittens that his cat had delivered and wanted them destroyed—all because he was too lazy to get his cat neutered."

"What'd you do?"

"I took them home with me and peddled them door to door. I think every neighbor in my entire apartment building had a cat or two by the time I was done."

"What did you do about the idiot with the prolific cat?"

"The third time he came in, I told him in no uncertain terms that if he didn't have his cat neutered, he could find himself another vet."

"And what did he say to that?"

"Not much, but he brought his cat in."

"That's something, I guess. What time is it, Sebastian?"

"About five-thirty."

"Would you mind if I cut out now? I promised Gran I'd fix the pineapple casserole. You want to come about six-thirty?"

"Six-thirty sounds fine."

He shouldn't have agreed to dinner, but it was too late to back out now. Besides, his telephone wasn't due to be hooked up until tomorrow, so he couldn't call to cancel. At least that's what he told himself. He did have to admit that a home-cooked meal was very appealing . . . not to mention a certain sun-blond sprite.

Was it possible that he'd been too hard on Danni? Just because she dressed in a less than conventional manner and talked a little fast didn't necessarily mean she was flighty or irresponsible. Did it? After all, she'd actually been quite a help today.

He opened a can of beef stew—people stew—for the cat who still refused to eat regular cat food. Sebastian, who'd showered and changed, watched the cat who, despite his size and ragtag appearance, ate fastidiously.

Sebastian left about twenty after six. To his surprise, the cat followed him out the door and walked beside him the whole way. He was still beside him when Sebastian arrived at Danni's.

She opened the door immediately. "Hi. Long time, no see."

Sebastian entered, and the cat sauntered along beside him as if he'd been invited in, as well.

Danni never batted an eye. She simply called over her shoulder, "Gran, could you please shut the door to the sun room?" She turned back to Sebastian. "Lewis and Carroll are out there."

Lewis again. "Oh, I didn't know you had other company."

"They're not company." Danni fluttered her lashes. "They live here."

"Family?"

"My mynah birds. I named them after the author of my favorite childhood story. *Alice in Wonderland.*"

That didn't surprise Sebastian at all. He'd already pegged her as Alice. "I don't know what's gotten into that cat." He looked around. "So where did the old reprobate take off to?"

Danni pointed to the hearth in front of the fireplace where the cat sat unconcerned on the rug and groomed his fur. "I hope he's not expecting a fire. He'll have to wait out a long, hot summer first."

"Do you want me to put him out?"

"Just leave him. He's fine there. Dinner will be ready in a minute. Can I get you something to drink? We have soft drinks, lemonade, and coffee."

It had been warm for an April day, so Sebastian opted for the lemonade, sipping the cold, tart liquid gratefully as he watched Danni fuss over a few last-minute details in the kitchen. He'd just now realized she'd changed clothes. A series of tank tops, one on top of the other, in blue, green, and yellow, topped baggy green satin trunks over orange biker's shorts. The color combination was so striking that Sebastian wondered how in the world he hadn't noticed it right off.

"I see you're not wearing pink and purple tonight," he murmured.

"Oh, but I am. A pink camisole and purple satin pant—" She broke off abruptly, as if realizing what she'd been about to say. "Um, you, um, look very nice." She indicated his khaki trousers and cream shirt. "Gran should be out shortly. The Women's Missionary Society lunch ran long today, so she's running a little late."

Sebastian barely heard her last sentence, his mind occupied instead with pink camisoles and purple satin panties. He could picture her all too clearly—her shapely legs highlighted by high-cut panties, the silky fabric of the camisole softly caressing her— He took a deep breath and looked at her beautiful hair. It was constrained in a more sedate braid. Somehow all he could think of was undoing that cool rope strand by polished strand. He'd spread that lush curtain over her shoulders so it would cascade down over the pink camisole and then—

"Sebastian?" Danni's soft voice interrupted his thoughts. "I'd like you to meet my grandmother, Virgie Pace."

Her grandmother wasn't at all the sweet, plump white-haired lady he was expecting. This was the grandmother who baked cookies and tended the roses by the front door? She looked more like Easy Rider's grandmother. She was small and wiry, and her short hair was a brilliant carrot orange underneath the black leather hat perched on top.

She wore a leather skirt with matching jacket and black boots and had four earrings in each ear. Sebastian's gaze lingered on the hat. Well, the Mad Hatter was an appropriate grandmother for Alice.

He smiled at the thought and extended his hand. "Hi, I'm Sebastian Kent. It's—it's a pleasure to meet you." He noticed Danni's look of amusement, as if she were used to this reaction to dear ol' Gran, and he found himself shooting her a look that promised retribution at the first available opportunity.

Virgie Pace took charge in the kitchen like a drill sergeant. "Sebastian, why don't you finish setting the table? And, Danielle, why don't you slice the ham? You're the only one who can get it thin enough."

Danielle? Sebastian shot a glance at her. Danielle suited her much better than Danni. Even in her layered tops and shorts, she still exuded femininity. Her curves were too pronounced and her features too delicate to be anything but feminine.

Despite her unconventional appearance, Virgie Pace *was* a good cook, he admitted as he ate generous helpings of ham, pineapple casserole, and the last of the peas from her backyard garden. And she was also good company as she chattered on about the town, the people, the weather. She slid from one topic to another without pause, and Sebastian found himself thoroughly entertained by her monologue. He could see where Danni got her unconventional manner—from Virgie's side of the family.

After dinner, Danni showed him around her home. Her surroundings revealed a lot about her. The sun room was obviously her place. The sofa was a swirl of soft pastel colors—including pink and purple—and gauzy pink curtains hung from the windows. It was such a feminine room that he should have felt out of place, but he didn't. He found the room warm and comfortable.

White wicker-and-glass shelves held a collection of figurines. When Sebastian stepped closer, he saw they were all fantasy creatures—wizards, fairies, unicorns, leprechauns.

"The only thing you're missing is Santa Claus and the Easter Bunny," he murmured, as he admired a tiny pewter unicorn.

Danni held up a porcelain rabbit with an amethyst egg in its paws. "Easter Bunny."

"Do you believe in all these?" Sebastian asked curiously.

She smiled that extraordinary, enigmatic smile.

"You mean, do I believe in leprechauns, unicorns, and fairies? Sure I do."

"How about magic?"

"Yes. Do you?"

"No. I've never seen any evidence of it."

"That's funny. I see it all the time." Danni sat in one corner of the sofa, drawing her legs beneath her.

Sebastian sat next to her and stretched out his long legs in front. "What do you mean?"

"I see magic everywhere. In everything. Every time I hear a baby laugh, or see a new foal struggle to its feet, when I see a rainbow or a sunset or a falling star. There's magic in every unexpected cool breeze on a hot day and in every rosebud that opens."

Sebastian inclined his head in acknowledgment. "But what about real magic, Danielle? You know, vanishing and reappearing, casting spells—"

"Love potions?" Danni watched as Sebastian squirmed a little.

"Yeah. That too."

"I've never seen any evidence that they *can't* happen."

"And I've never seen any evidence that they *can.*"

"So you only believe in what you see?"

"That's right."

Danni sighed. "How sad. Tell me, do you believe dinosaurs existed?"

"Of course." Sebastian raised an eyebrow, wondering where this conversation was leading. "Why? Have you ever seen one?"

"Well no, but—"

"Then, by your definition, you can't believe in them."

"But there's plenty of evidence that they have existed."

A smug smile curved Danni's lips. "So there is. And there's plenty of evidence that magic exists."

"Not that I've seen."

"Then you haven't been looking with the right eyes," Danni retorted mildly.

"These are the only eyes I have," he said in heated defense. "What do you suggest I do? Go buy another pair?" He grinned. "That sounds ridiculous, doesn't it?"

A surge of melting warmth curled in Danni's stomach, and she smiled back. "Oh, I don't know. You might try Bosco Wilson's Food Mart. He carries everything else." She paused a moment. "Sebastian, if you looked at things with your heart—"

"I tried that once," he muttered, more to himself than her. "It got handed back to me in pieces."

"What do you mean?" Danni asked, but knew he wouldn't answer. She had seen the shutters go up, blocking out some painful memory, and she wished with all her heart she could ease his hurt.

He rose from the sofa and walked over to the large wicker birdcage in the corner. "Which one's Lewis and which one's Carroll?"

Danni could tell he was trying to change the subject. With any luck there'd be time enough to learn what—or who—had caused him pain. "Lewis is the one trying to bite you." She indicated the bird clinging to the side of the cage.

"Ouch! What do you mean 'trying'? Why didn't you tell me he could get his head through the bars?" He held up his forefinger with a barely discernible red mark on it. "So," he said sternly, though with laughter in his eyes, "you're raising vicious, man-eating birds."

Danni opened the door to the cage and put her hand in. Lewis, as gingerly as though he were walking on pins, stepped onto her wrist. When she drew the bird out, she brought up her other hand, and Lewis butted his head against it like a cat asking to be petted. Danni scratched him gently on his breast plumage, and he half-closed his eyes in bliss. "See? He's nothing but a baby."

"Yeah, well, that 'baby' is teething," Sebastian said, trying unsuccessfully to hide a grin. "Does he talk?"

"Not yet. He's the strong, silent type, I guess. Carroll's the real chatterbox." Danni bent down to coo softly at the other bird.

He still couldn't figure her out, he thought as he watched her. She had the same impish sense of humor as one of those leprechauns she professed to believe in. And she apparently looked at life as one great adventure. He couldn't help but wonder if she'd bring that same sense of adventure into the bedroom.

Would she approach making love with the same creativity and innovation with which she approached everything else? Would she be as confusing and mercurial? Or would she approach making love with certainty and precision? Who would she be in the bedroom—that innocent, amused sprite of their first meeting or the warm, vibrant woman of their second?

These were dangerous thoughts, he realized, as he felt the unmistakable surge of desire. He walked over to the window and pulled back the curtain to peer out into the huge backyard. What he saw took him aback. "Is that . . . ?"

"A pig sleeping on the back porch?" Danni came over to stand next to him. "Yes. That's Marigold. She's Gran's pet. She was one of Mrs. Walling's. The runt of the litter. That's why she's not very big."

Nothing about this family should surprise him after this, Sebastian thought. "Your grandmother certainly is, well, unconventional, isn't she?"

Danni gave another one of her aggravating smiles. "Is she?"

"So, have you lived here all your life?"

"Oh, no. I was born in Raleigh. My parents still live there, as a matter of fact. I came up here when I went to college the first time, then decided to stay and get my second degree. I used to spend summers here though. It's a great town for a kid."

"Do you plan to marry and settle down here?"

"Gracious, no! I have dreams—big dreams. When I finish up at the end of May, I intend to set up practice in some really exotic locale. Bermuda, maybe. Hawaii. Australia. I've got a whole world to see. I don't know if I'll ever get married. Marriage and babies seem to tie women down. They don't seem to slow down men, usually, but then, men don't have to get pregnant."

"That's true enough," Sebastian murmured.

"I don't ever want to be referred to as the little woman or the old lady or, God forbid, the old ball and chain." She looked at Sebastian curiously. "What about you, Sebastian? Would you ever call your wife any of those things?"

"I . . . it's getting late. I should be going. When do you think we should go see the lady with the cats?"

"Magda's pretty flexible. How about if we plan on Thursday about one? I'll pick you up."

"Pick me up?"

"Since you don't know where she lives, I thought it might be easier if I drove."

God only knows how she drives, Sebastian thought, and insisted, "I'll drive, and you can give me directions."

"Sebastian, Magda lives on a dirt road. Do you have a four-wheel drive?"

"Well, no—"

"So I'll drive. I have a sturdy little Jeep that'll get me anywhere I have to go."

Then, as if she'd known what he'd been thinking, she added, "I'm an excellent driver. So, Thursday at one it is. I'll see you tomorrow morning."

"Sure thing."

Wednesday went pretty much the way Tuesday had gone. Despite his earlier reservations about having Danni work for him, things went well. Very well. Even though she dressed, looked, and talked as if she were flighty, even irresponsible, Sebastian began to realize that beneath it all she had a shrewd intelligence and keen wit and, amazingly enough, well-organized work habits.

While he treated his animal patients, she quietly observed his procedures, asking the occasional pointed question. In between, she studied.

At the end of the day he glanced through the billing system she'd set up and found it extremely efficient. Okay, so he'd been wrong about some things. She wasn't featherheaded. But he still doubted her staying power. How long before she'd get bored working here and want to move on?

For that matter he wondered if she'd manage to stick out her classes, then decided she would. Whatever else she might be, she genuinely liked working with animals—and was damned good at it too. He almost hated to admit it, but based on what he'd seen these past two days, she'd make a fine vet—if she could stay in one place long enough to establish a practice.

After she'd left for the day, Sebastian leaned his back against the door for a moment and looked around the room. His house seemed so lifeless, so lonely, after she'd gone. And the loneliness lingered after Sebastian went to bed.

He'd kept it at bay while he'd read the latest veterinary journal and watched a couple of hours of television, but once he turned out the light, it pressed down on him. He turned the light back on and lay in bed looking around the room. It was a much larger bedroom than he'd had in his posh New York apartment, and it had a big bay window overlooking a beautiful, if neglected, flower garden.

It was light and airy, but Sebastian couldn't help but feel it was sterile, with none of the bright colors and contrasting textures that made Danni's home so warm and memorable. Or was it the colors and textures that made it warm and memorable? No, it was Danni herself, with her effervescent laughter and aura of restless energy. Even when she sat perfectly still, the very air seemed to vibrate around her. All she had to do was walk into a room for it to seem to come to life.

Somehow, thinking about Danni now made his loneliness all the more intense. Funny, he'd been alone for the past four years—ever since Sharon—but he hadn't been lonely. Not until Danni.

The two women were so different, yet so alike. Sharon, too, had been a butterfly. But instead of flitting from topic to topic, like Danni, she'd flitted from job to job, from man to man. Of course, when he'd been married to her, he hadn't known about the other men—not until she'd wound up pregnant. No, not until she had the baby, he corrected himself. She'd actually let him go through the pregnancy with her, excited and happy. He could still remember the surge of joy that had shot through him when they'd placed the baby in his arms.

And he could still remember the stabs of anguish when he'd learned that the baby, that beautiful tiny little girl, wasn't his. Sharon wasn't even sure whether it belonged to José, her tennis instructor, or Marcus, her current employer, until they'd all had blood tests.

So hadn't he learned not to get involved with butterflies? Hadn't he learned the hard way?

It was closer to one-thirty than one on Thursday when Danni pulled up in front of Sebastian's. "Sorry," she apologized as soon as she'd pulled up in the driveway. "Some idiot double-parked beside me at school, and I had trouble getting out."

"That's all right. I wouldn't have been ready earlier, anyway. I just had a committee of blue-haired ladies bring by enough food to feed the combined marching bands of the army, navy, and marines."

"The Missionary Society. Gran must have told them you were all settled in. Are you ready now? Do you have everything? Where's your cat?"

"He's not my cat, and I don't know where he is. He decided not to follow me home last night.

He didn't show up this morning for breakfast either."

"There he is." Danni pointed to his front window where the cat sat sunning himself—on the inside.

"How did he get in?"

"Oh, cats can always find a way in. I wonder how well he'll ride."

Sebastian opened the house door, and the cat came out and walked straight over to the Jeep, hopping in the middle of the front seat. He unconcernedly began to groom himself as Sebastian tossed his bag in the back and got in beside him.

"You certainly have a strange cat," Danni commented as she backed out into the street.

"He's not my cat." The cat, apparently deciding to make a liar out of Sebastian, crawled into his lap and sat looking out the side window.

"You may be right. He's not so much your cat as you're his human." She grinned.

Sebastian snorted. "That's true enough. I don't seem to have any say in the matter."

He studied Danni as she drove. More pink and purple. She wore a pink-and-purple-striped T-shirt, blue jeans with pink and purple daisies embroidered down the sides, and pink sneakers. She looked adorable . . . and sexy. He turned his head toward the window, sure that the sanest thing to do would be to not look at her at all.

She drove past the post office, the store, the gas station, and the diner that made up the heart of town and headed out Denning Lane. Sebastian commented on the wide carpets of yellow, red, pink, and blue wildflowers that extended down either side of the road. "This is beautiful."

"Thank you. It took most of last summer to accomplish, but I'm pleased with the way it turned out."

"You did this?" He'd already seen at her house last night that color and beauty were important to her. Apparently, she wanted to extend that color and beauty to everyone around her.

"The whole town did it. I simply suggested the project at the town council last spring. I thought it would be prettier to look at wildflowers than banks of half-dead grass."

"It's a shame more towns don't do something like this." If they had Danni spearheading their projects, he thought, they would.

Danni turned onto a narrow dirt road and came to a stop.

"What's wrong?" Sebastian asked, then saw the answer to his question. Four cats slept in the middle of the road. "I take it we're close to Magda's house?"

Danni nodded and got out of the Jeep, shooed the cats away, then got back in and continued another twenty yards or so before having to stop to repeat the procedure. In between cat-chasing stops, she tried to avoid the dozens of puddles and ruts in the road but managed to hit a few anyway. Every time she did, she let out a cheerful string of epithets that had Sebastian grinning. Some he'd never even heard before. Even her language was exceedingly colorful.

When he saw Magda's house, the grin faded, replaced by awe. For some reason he'd pictured a log cabin and Magda as a wizened old woman, dispensing potions and advice to the locals. But her house was a huge Dutch Colonial with columns across the front and stone lions on either side of the walk. It looked for all the world like a scaled-down plantation.

Danni pursed her lips when she saw his face. "Not quite what you were expecting, is it?"

"Hey, I didn't say—"

"You didn't have to. Anyway, I'd better prepare you for Magda. She's not quite what you'd expect either."

"You're enjoying this, aren't you?"

With an effort she bit back a laugh. "Darn right! You city folks come into a small town and right away want to fit everyone into a mold. Well, here in White Creek nobody fits into a mold."

Sebastian sighed good-naturedly. "Okay, so prepare me."

"She's sort of a cross between Katharine Hepburn and"—she paused for a moment, her brow creased, then she smiled—"and Popeye."

"Katharine Hepburn and Popeye?"

"You'll understand when you meet her. Here she comes now."

The woman who opened the front door of the house was tall and elegant like Katharine Hepburn. But on closer inspection one could see the bulging forearms like Popeye, as well as the corncob pipe clutched in her teeth.

"She doesn't really smoke it," Danni murmured, then turned, and held out her hand. "Hello, Magda."

"This the new vet?" Magda asked in a gravelly voice.

"Yes. This is Dr. Kent. Sebastian, this is Magda Jones."

He offered his hand, and Magda squeezed it firmly while she gave him a piercing look. "You should wear blue. Be a good color for you."

"I don't wear much blue." *And I'll certainly make a special effort to avoid it now.*

"Well, I take it you came to vaccinate my cats, so I'll call them."

She let out a loud whistle, and within minutes, cats of all shapes, sizes, and colors began showing up. They wrapped themselves around Magda's ankles until she seemed to be wading in a sea of fur.

When Sebastian went back to the Jeep to get his bag, he saw his cat curled up in the middle of the front seat, sleeping. "Magda? Is he one of your cats?"

Magda came over and peered in the window. "Never saw him before. Odd cat. Got six toes on his back paw. See that? Does he have one blue eye and one green eye?"

"As a matter of fact, he does. Do you know where he belongs?"

"Nope. Just that my grandma—she was a Gypsy, you know—always said that a six-toed cat with two-color eyes is special, so I'd be on the lookout for something extraordinary to happen."

To Sebastian's way of thinking, something extraordinary had already happened. He'd found Alice and the Mad Hatter alive and well in White Creek, Virginia.

THREE

All the cats were examined and vaccinated in a relatively short period of time, all things considered. Somehow Danni knew each and every cat, its age, and medical history. Sebastian didn't know how she did it, but if it hadn't been for her, he'd have become totally confused. He had to admit Danni was truly amazing.

It was late afternoon before they arrived back at Sebastian's. Magda had served them an elegantly prepared, if unconventional, lunch of sardine-and-spinach sandwiches. Lunch had taken quite a while, because they had spent more time shooing away the cats than eating.

"Is there anything I can help you with before I go home?" Danni asked.

For a moment, just a moment, Sebastian was

tempted to think up some busywork so he'd have more time with her. "I'm not going to do anything else today, but thanks for offering."

"Any time. What are assistants for?"

Sebastian just smiled. "Good night, Danni."

"Good night, Sebastian. I'll see you tomorrow."

When he opened the Jeep door, the cat jumped out of his lap, ran across the lawn, up the tree next to the house, and leapt onto the porch roof. "What got into him?" Sebastian rubbed his thigh where the cat's sharp claws had left their mark.

"I guess he was eager to get out of the Jeep. He did spend most of the day in here."

"By choice. I tried to take him out at Magda's, and he jumped back in the window."

"Maybe he thought you were going to leave him there."

"I don't know why he'd think that. So far he's done exactly what *he* wants to do, regardless of what I want."

"He is an independent thing, isn't he?" They watched him as he paced back and forth across the porch roof, meowing. "I wonder why he's crying? Do you suppose he can't figure out how to get down?"

"He got up there and all by himself."

"Come on, Sebastian. You're a vet. You know

that animals often get into places they can't get out of."

Sebastian swung his legs out of the Jeep and stretched in the late-afternoon sun. "So what do you want me to do about it?" He figured she'd tell him.

"I think you should try to get him down."

He knew it. "And how should I do that?"

"Got a ladder?"

"In the toolshed in back. But I . . . I'm afraid of heights."

Danni rolled her eyes. "Figures."

"I'll go upstairs and open a window. Maybe I can get him in that way."

Danni hopped out of the Jeep. "Okay. Let's go."

"That's all right. I can manage."

"Have you realized that you spend an awful lot of time trying to convince me you don't need my help?"

"It's a waste of time, isn't it? You don't listen to me any more than the cat does."

"Not about that I don't." Danni followed him upstairs, filled with curiosity about his room. What would it reveal about the man?

It didn't reveal much, she thought in disappointment when they walked down the hall. From the glimpse she'd gotten, it seemed tastefully furnished but bland. No pictures, no plants, no personal effects. Maybe he hadn't unpacked them yet. Or maybe he'd left them behind in New York. But why? Was there something about New York he wanted to forget?

Sebastian went to an empty room at the end of the hall. "This one overlooks the porch. Let's see if he'll make it easy on everyone and come in." He opened the window and leaned out. "Here, kitty."

Danni peered over Sebastian's shoulder. The cat sat just out of reach, watching the two of them. She could have sworn there was a gleam of amusement in its mismatched eyes.

Sebastian continued to call the cat, and it continued to sit and watch him. Finally, Sebastian said, "I'll leave the window open so he can come in whenever he's ready. Okay?" He turned around, catching Danni off-guard. Their faces were no more than four inches apart. Danni was mesmerized by the walnut-brown eyes inches from hers. What happened to the oxygen? she wondered as she stepped back.

Her brain seemed to be working sluggishly. "I, uh, I'll see you tomorrow then. Nine?"

He nodded. "About Saturday, what office hours will people expect?"

"On Saturdays, they'll expect house calls. As a matter of fact, I already have a list of several house calls for you to make."

"You have a list?"

"Sure. Everybody in town knows I'm your assistant, so they've been calling me. After all, your phone isn't even hooked up yet."

"They're supposed to get to that late this afternoon."

Danni headed back down the stairs. "That means it'll be any time between now and whenever. If you want to leave my phone number with anyone, feel free."

"No. There's no one."

At the front door Danni turned to face him. "No family or friends?" Danni didn't consider herself a nosy person, but she'd have given almost anything to know what it was that had chased Sebastian out of New York. And she was convinced that that was what had happened. He hadn't given up a successful practice in Manhattan to come to White Creek and vaccinate cats. No, it was more that he'd *escaped* to White Creek.

"There's no one."

Danni couldn't quite let it drop. "What about your parents?"

"They're currently celebrating their fortieth wedding anniversary somewhere in the Caribbean. And if they have nothing better to do than call me, then they've got problems."

He opened the door for her, and she walked

out onto the porch. "Oh. Well, if you change your mind . . ." She let her words trail off.

"Thanks. And thanks for taking me out to Magda's. It was"—he grinned—"an experience."

Sebastian walked her to the Jeep and held her door for her. She climbed in, giving him a high-wattage smile. "An experience. That sums up Magda pretty well. And you."

"Me?"

Danni looked at him, her violet-blue eyes clear and direct. "Meeting you has been an experience, Dr. Kent. A very pleasant experience. I'm glad you came here. You're a special man."

She watched as Sebastian opened his mouth to say something, then shut it again. What kind of idiots had he left behind in New York that they hadn't ever said that to him? He turned and walked slowly to the front porch, while Danni stared thoughtfully at his back. When he'd reached the top step, he looked back at her.

Danni fumbled with her car keys a moment before fitting them into the ignition. Sebastian watching her made her nervous. She finally got the Jeep started and looked up to wave at him, only he was no longer standing on the top step. He was lying on the bottom step.

"Omigosh! Omigosh!" Danni scrambled out of the Jeep and ran over to him. He lay still, the only color to his suddenly pale face the reddened swelling that was rising rapidly on his right temple. It was easy to figure out what had happened. The cat sat on the porch roof, right over where Sebastian had stood, and a piece of the slate roof lay next to Sebastian's head on the step. The cat must have dislodged the shingle; it fell and knocked Sebastian out.

Danni's brain rapidly sifted through all the first-aid tidbits she'd collected over the years. *Elevate feet. Yes, she should do that. Check for bleeding*. She looked him over carefully. There wasn't much. Just a little smear of blood on his right temple.

Okay, what else? Keep him warm. A blanket. A pillow and a blanket. She raced upstairs and grabbed the blanket and one of the pillows from his bed. She placed the pillow under his feet and covered him with the blanket. *Call the doctor.*

" 'S too hot for that," Sebastian mumbled, and brushed the blanket away as he propped himself up on one elbow. "What happened?"

"Oh, God, you're conscious. You're conscious." Danni brushed away the moisture in her eyes. "Stay still, okay? I'm going to dash next door and call the doctor. I'll be right back."

"No. I'm fine." He sat up shakily.

"Sebastian, please lie down," she pleaded. "You might have a concussion or something."

"I'm fine," he insisted, and struggled to his feet, hanging on to the porch railing. He hastily sat down again, dropping his head into his hands.

"I knew it! I'm going to call the doctor."

"Forget it! I'm fine."

"Do you know who I am? Where you are? What's your name? Do you know your name?"

"You're Alice, this is Wonderland, and my name is the March Hare."

Danni blanched. "I'm getting the doctor."

"Bad joke. You're Danni, this is White Creek, and my name is Sebastian. I told you, I am fine. My head hurts a little, that's all. What happened, anyway?"

"I'm not sure, but I think the cat knocked one of those old slate tiles loose, and it slid down on your head. Do you hurt anywhere else?"

Without thinking, she sat next to him and ran her hands down his ribs searching for a fracture. Not that she'd recognize one if she felt it, but she couldn't do nothing. The yielding firmness of muscles beneath her fingers made her wonder about his chest. Did he have a lot of hair or just a little? Would it be springy to the touch or silky? *Oh, this is horrible. I can't be thinking this. He needs a doctor, for Pete's sake!*

Sebastian grasped her wrists, stilling her hands on his chest. "I'm fine, Danielle. I need to lie down a little while. That's all. Would you mind helping me upstairs?"

"No. No, of course not, but I'd really feel better if you'd let me call Dr.—"

"It would waste his time. He'd tell me to go to bed, which I'm going to do right now. He'd tell you to put an ice bag on my head, which you'll do as soon as I get in bed. Then he'd tell you to wake me up every hour or two and make sure I know what day it is and who you are, and he'd tell you to watch for nausea. And you'll do that, won't you?"

Danni nodded. "Of course I will. But I'd still feel better calling the doctor."

"Why bother the man?" He tried standing again, this time with more success, though he held on to the porch railing with both hands. As he turned to go inside, he glanced up at the cat, peering over the side of the roof. "Magda was right about one thing. She said that cat would mean something extraordinary. And it did. It damn near killed me."

"Don't even say that as a joke!" Danni said as she wrapped a helping arm around his middle.

His head hurt like hell, and he was beginning to identify aches in other parts of his body that would likely develop into bruises later. But he wasn't in so much pain that he failed to notice how well they fit together even though he was quite a bit taller than she. She seemed so delicate, but she was much stronger than she looked, he realized, as he felt the strength of her arm around his waist.

He could rest his cheek against the top of her head and breathe in the light, sweet fragrance of her hair. He could feel the curve of her body next to him and the way her breast brushed lightly against his arm. And he could remember in vivid detail how her hands had felt on his chest moments before. The sudden throb of desire in his loins was counteracted by a stab of pain from his head. He sat down hard on the edge of the bed.

Danni dropped to her knees in front of him and eased his shoes off. "Lie down now. Please."

"I want to take off my shirt. Don't want to get it too wrinkled. I hate to iron." He dropped the shirt on the floor and with a groan let his head sink into his blessedly soft pillow.

"What's wrong?" Danni asked quickly. "Do you want me to get the doctor?"

"Everything's fine. It just feels good to lie down, that's all. Stop worrying about me, Danielle. I'm fine. Really."

"I don't know. I don't feel right about this. You might have really injured yourself. Let me look at your eyes."

"What for?"

"Uneven pupils. I think that's a sign of a concussion."

He opened his eyes but said, "It's not necessary. My pupils are even."

She bent close and peered into his eyes. "They do look okay, but I'll have to check them later on, too, in case something shows up."

"If that will make you happy."

"It will. I'm going downstairs to get the blanket I left on your steps and some ice. I'll be back in a minute. Don't try to get up."

He hated hearing that worried tone in her voice, and he contemplated calling her back to reassure her that it wasn't all that bad. He'd had bumps far worse than this, and his head didn't even hurt much as long as he stayed still, but he remained silent. And he wasn't sure why. Was it that he *liked* her fussing over him? It certainly was a change.

During his dreary, difficult marriage to Sharon, he'd always had to be the nurturer. She'd needed a lot of emotional support, even babying. In retrospect, he could see he probably hadn't done her any favors by bailing her out and wiping her tears. He should have encouraged her to grow up and accept responsibility for herself.

Of course, he'd had a lot of practice in taking care of other people. His parents had been so wrapped up in their careers that they'd often forgotten things—like making house payments, paying the utility bills, buying groceries. From the time he'd been old enough to understand the words "Past Due," he'd taken on the responsibility of paying the bills, bringing the checks to his parents for their signatures.

He didn't hold any grudges against his parents—he loved them, and he understood their preoccupation with their careers. Even as a child, he'd been proud of them; his mother was a microbiologist, his father a historian. And he'd known they loved him. Still, he could remember more than one childhood illness when he'd fixed his own orange juice and chicken soup and put himself to bed. Somehow chicken pox or measles hadn't been important enough to command their full attention.

And yet here was Miss Danielle Sullivan tucking a blanket around him, then gently brushing his hair back from his forehead before putting an ice bag on the place where the shingle had struck.

"Can I get you anything?" she asked. "Do you want something to drink? Maybe something cold?"

"That would be nice. I have some canned juice in one of the kitchen cabinets."

"*Canned?*" Danni wrinkled her nose. "I don't think so. I'll be back in a flash. You close your eyes while I'm gone, okay?" She watched him. "Close 'em."

"You'll be quick?" Okay, so his voice sounded a little weaker than necessary, he thought guiltily. But he'd had a head injury and shouldn't be alone more than a few minutes.

Danni laid her hand on his arm. "I'll be right back. I promise. Now, please close your eyes and rest for a few minutes."

He complied. Her scent hovered, compelling even in her absence. His eyelids drifted shut as he tried to put a name to the fragrance.

. . . In just a minute she was back. Only now her braid had been loosened, her golden hair flowing down over her arms. He was disappointed he hadn't been the one to undo that braid. She'd changed clothes, too, and now wore purple—one of those lacy things they called teddies. He called it delightful, decadent, delectable. It bared her beautiful creamy legs—legs surprisingly long for a petite woman. The thin, silky fabric displayed her firm, full breasts and hardened nipples to his heated gaze.

She came toward him, her fragrance floating out to greet him—the sun-warmed scent of summer roses—and he closed his eyes to savor it. He felt her weight settle next to him on the bed and opened his eyes again.

It was the cat. "Meow." The cat touched his nose to Sebastian's.

Sebastian sighed. "Damn cat. You weren't sure the shingle had done the job, so you came up here to finish it, huh?"

He heard footsteps running up the stairs, and Danni dashed in the door. "I'm back," she panted. "Are you okay? Here's your juice. I went home for it. Fresh-squeezed. Gran made it just this morning. I also brought a plate of food to heat up for your supper later."

Sebastian took the glass of orange juice and brought it to his lips for a sip. The cat, at the same time, decided to check out the liquid and nearly stuck his nose in Sebastian's mouth. Sebastian sighed again. "Look, cat, why don't you go climb a tree or, better yet, catch a mouse or two, will ya?" The cat immediately jumped off the bed and headed out the bedroom door.

"What was that all about?" Danni asked.

"If that cat would spend more time doing his catly duty and less time creating trouble for me, it would be better for everybody." He drained half the glass in one gulp. "This is good. Thanks."

Danni took the half-empty glass from him and set it on the nightstand. "Why don't you try to sleep a little while?" She brushed her fingers across the raised welt on his temple, then gently adjusted the position of the ice bag. "How's that? Does it feel okay?" When he nodded, she added,

"I'll wake you in about an hour or so to make sure you're all right."

Sebastian obediently closed his eyes, and Danni picked up the veterinary journal from the floor next to the bed and spent the next hour flipping through it. She kept glancing at Sebastian. He looked different when he slept. The lines that seemed so much a part of his forehead were erased, and with his sardonic, shadowed eyes closed, he seemed almost innocent—like a young boy.

Of course, this boyish image was immediately belied by the firm male chest revealed by the blanket that he had kicked off in his sleep. Danni caught her breath at the sheer beauty of it. She'd never before paid much attention to the human body, neither hers nor anyone else's. Although she could remember a time in early adolescence when she'd bemoaned the soft curves that had suddenly begun to attract so many grasping adolescent males.

But Sebastian's body seemed extraordinarily well put together. A broad tan muscled chest tapered into narrow hips and muscular thighs. Each part, taken by itself, was terrific enough. Together they were magnificent. The veterinary journal slipped unnoticed from her lap onto the floor as she stood and sat next to him on the edge of the bed. She reached out one finger and traced the thin white line of a jagged scar that curved up over the left side of his collarbone. She wondered what had happened. It looked old, as if it came from a childhood accident.

Did he climb trees as a boy, or play baseball, or perform daredevil stunts on his bike? Had he been the kind of active, afraid-of-nothing kid who both delighted and frightened his parents?

Danielle smiled at the thought of Sebastian as a little boy and ran gentle fingers over a reddened area on his left side that was already beginning to darken into an impressive bruise. He must have landed on his ribs when he fell. At least it didn't feel swollen or otherwise unusual to the touch, so maybe he'd escaped breaking a rib.

She found her fingertips lightly tracing around a brown curl. It was soft to the touch. Well, that was one question answered. Unfortunately, she had thousands more about him. She wondered how he kissed. His lips were so firm and well-shaped, would they be soft to kiss or would they harden in passion? She was surprised to find that her hand had flattened against his warm, tanned skin.

He stirred and moaned, then brought up one hand and encircled her wrist, holding her hand against his chest. He opened his eyes.

"Oh, I'm so sorry. Did I hurt you?" She stared down at her hand, noticing that her fingers had threaded through the curls on his chest. Now when had that happened?

"No." At the husky sound of his voice, Danni's gaze met his, seeing the sudden hunger flare in his golden-brown eyes. His gaze dropped to her parted lips as his hand left her wrist and slid up her arm to her shoulder, leaving every inch of skin tingling. His fingers brushed over the hollow of her throat, then wrapped around the back of her neck, urging her head down.

No. Oh, this isn't a good idea, Danni thought. *We've known each other only a few days*. But the minute their lips met, she lost all thoughts of resisting. Their mouths fit together perfectly, his warm and firm, hers soft and yielding. It started so innocently, his lips barely moving against hers, caressing, coaxing. Gradually, the pressure increased, and his tongue teased her lips apart. Caught up in his taste, she opened her mouth to his, and the tip of his tongue boldly moved in.

Danni's hands slid from his chest to his shoulders, and a small sound, part protest, part surrender, left her lips as the weight of her body melted full against him. She had stopped thinking that they hardly knew each other. She had even stopped thinking that it felt so right. She had stopped thinking at all. One lone warning bell rang in the far recesses of her mind, and although she couldn't have said why, she made a barely discernible effort to push herself away.

It was enough. Sebastian's lips gentled, then stilled, and she leaned back, brushing a strand of hair from her face with a shaky hand. Their gazes met again, and Danni noticed that he looked as shell-shocked as she felt.

"I, ah, I'll go heat up your dinner," she murmured. When she'd thought about kissing him, she hadn't realized it would be like this. She'd been thinking along the lines of pleasant, good—great, even. She hadn't considered earthshaking.

Sebastian drew in a deep breath and glanced at the clock. "It's too early for dinner. Danielle—"

"Then I'll go put some more ice in the ice bag."

"I don't want more ice. Danielle—"

"Look, Sebastian," she interrupted, "I—this, this was a mistake. I don't want—"

"I agree."

She looked at him for a long moment, then repeated, "You agree?"

"I agree. I don't believe in getting involved with people I work with, for one. And I'm not in the market to get involved with anyone right now." *Especially an utterly charming and all-too-appealing Alice in Wonderland type.*

Danni sighed in relief. "Me either."

"We'll both need to make sure this doesn't happen again."

"Absolutely. It can't happen again. It could complicate our working relationship."

"Immeasurably. And I don't think either one of us needs that."

She gave a patently false smile. "Well, then, why don't you try to sleep a little longer? I'll go downstairs and find something to do—clean up or something." She walked to the door of the room.

"Danielle?" he called after her. "Please don't try to organize anything. I mean, I have my own system."

She nodded brusquely and left the room.

Sebastian stared after her. He'd meant everything he'd said. He didn't believe in getting involved with people he worked with. And he wasn't looking to get involved with anyone right now. Especially not with her. She had no staying power. She might not ever cheat on a man the way Sharon had, but she'd always be flitting off after another flower.

And yet, he didn't think it was going to be as easy as all that. Something had his libido bumping around like a bee in a bottle. Maybe it was the fresh country air or the celibacy he'd clung to the past four years. Or maybe it was

Danielle. Danielle with her pansy-violet eyes and silky sunny hair. And smile. That delicious smile that grabbed hold of a man and squeezed the breath out of him.

And those lips. Those heavenly lips. When he had felt her lips part beneath his and the sweet pressure of her body, he'd felt desire slam into him like a sledgehammer. The remnants of it still tingled along his spine. He knew one thing. Working with her was going to be difficult as hell.

He must have dozed again, because the next time Danni came into the room, it was nearly six-thirty. She carried a tray in her hands and set it on the nightstand.

"How do you feel?" she asked brightly, looking everywhere but at his eyes.

"Fine." He sat up, propping a pillow behind his back. He was relieved to note that his headache was gone, except for a little localized tenderness where the shingle had struck him. The desire hadn't gone though. It still shimmied along his nerve endings as he looked at Danni. "That smells good."

"Lemon chicken, glazed carrots from Magda's garden, snap beans from mine. I didn't know what you wanted to drink, so I fixed iced tea, but I can make coffee, if you'd prefer it. Or I can run home and get lemonade—"

"This is fine. Thank you." Lord, but this conversation was stilted. Before long they'd be chatting about the weather and somebody's gallbladder. This had to stop. "Danielle—" He paused, not sure what he wanted to say.

Just then the cat jumped up on the foot of the bed, and Sebastian thankfully turned his attention there instead. "So, you old rascal, where've you been this afternoon?"

"What's that in his mouth?"

"What?"

Danni pointed at a wiggling gray something, but before either of them could do anything, the cat blinked, then walked daintily up the length of the bed and deposited a mouse, a live mouse, in the middle of Sebastian's chest. Forever after, Danni would remember what happened next in disjointed images—Sebastian jumping up, the mouse scampering to freedom, the startled cat jumping onto the tray, chicken and vegetables flying everywhere.

When the commotion died down, Danni was rubbing her shin where the tray had clipped her and the cat sat in the corner feasting on lemon chicken. Sebastian wiped glazed carrots and beans from the nightstand and gave the cat a disgusted look.

"What the hell did he do that for?"

Danni looked up from the food stains on her jeans. "Do what for? Give you the mouse?"

"Yeah."

"He was doing what you asked him to do. Don't you remember?"

"What?"

"A little while ago you shooed him away and told him to go catch a mouse or two, didn't you?"

"Well, yeah, but—"

"So why are you surprised?"

"Danielle, you're talking as though he understood what I said."

"Suppose he did?"

"Don't be ridiculous. He was doing what any normal cat would do in a mouse-infested farmhouse. Cats catch mice. Period."

"You sure that's all there is to it? Magda said he was an extraordinary cat."

"And you believe everything she says?"

Danni just looked at him and said nothing.

"Stop looking at me," Sebastian muttered crossly. "Your eyes are doing it again."

"Doing what?"

"That sparkly thing."

"Are you all right?"

"Every time we discuss some questionable subject—like magic, for example—you get this strange look in your eyes . . . they . . . they twinkle at me."

Danni jumped to her feet. "That's it. I'm calling Dr. Hartman right now. I think you're hallucinating. Either that or you've slipped a cog."

"If I've slipped a cog, it's because you keep going on about—never mind. I'm just fine, Danielle. You don't need to call anyone."

"Then why are you saying these weird things about my eyes?"

Sebastian sighed and rubbed the back of his neck. "I'm only spouting off. What do you expect from a starving man who's watching his dinner being devoured by a four-footed menace?"

Danni jumped to her feet. "Oh, I'm sorry. You must have something to eat. How about if I clean up this mess and fix you something else?"

"Why don't you open a can or something? I'm so hungry that at this point I don't really care what it is."

The cat followed Danni downstairs. "He still doesn't believe in magic," she murmured to the cat, as she stopped to stroke his head. "And he needs to. So much."

FOUR

Danni threw together a quick meal out of what she could find in Sebastian's sparsely stocked kitchen. While he was eating, she scrubbed the food stains from the floor and wall. The cat sat on the windowsill, tail twitching and looking as if he were ready to pounce on the sponge as it swished back and forth.

Then followed one of the most uncomfortable two hours Danni had ever spent. She sat in the chair at the foot of the bed and pretended to read a magazine, while Sebastian lay in the bed and pretended to watch the television. She kept sneaking glances at him only to find that he was sneaking glances at her. Finally, about nine-thirty, she rose and laid the magazine on the nightstand.

"I guess I'll go now. I have some notes to

study for a makeup lab tomorrow. I'll run back over here before I go to bed to make sure you're all right." *Maybe that'll give me enough time to herd my hormones into a nice neat little package.*

"That's not necessary. My head doesn't even hurt anymore, and I'm certainly not nauseated." He kept looking at her with a curiously amused smile.

She looked away from his all too compelling gaze. "I don't mind, and I think I'd sleep better if I checked. I'll just leave your back door unlocked."

"Unlocked? Why don't you take my key?"

"Sebastian, this is White Creek. We don't lock our doors here."

"What about crime?"

"Crime? The last breaking-and-entering here was when the post-office door got stuck and Mrs. Heard climbed in the back window. And the last time anyone got arrested for anything was when Sam Johnston shot at old man Petrie's rooster because it kept crowing underneath his bedroom window."

Sebastian shook his head. "This is a far cry from New York. Back there, we had two sets of locks on every door and a burglar-alarm system."

"Is that why you moved here?"

"Part of the reason, maybe. Mostly, I needed

a change of scene. Besides, I was getting tired of treating neurotic poodles and pampered parakeets. I saw too many underexercised pets, too many overfed pets. I thought some nice normal hounds and the occasional cow or horse would be nice.

"I spent the summer I graduated veterinary school with a country vet in Connecticut. I really liked the small town, the animals, the easier pace. I didn't even mind getting paid in milk and eggs. So when I decided to leave New York after nearly eight years, I looked for the same kind of thing."

All that was only part of the reason he was here, she realized. There was something else. Something that caused looks of pain to cross his face. She needed to know what that something was. This was a puzzle she was going to have to put together one tiny little piece at a time.

"How long did you live in New York?" She kept her voice casual.

"Eight years. After the summer in Connecticut, I moved to New York to set up my practice."

"Where did you grow up?"

"Albany."

"Why didn't you set up your practice there?"

Because I'd just met Sharon, and she had one more year of college, and she didn't want to leave

New York. But he didn't explain to Danni; he merely shrugged.

"You, um, said that there was no one in New York who'd be needing to get in touch with you?"

Sebastian's expression hardened. "That's right. No one who'd dare even try." Even Sharon wouldn't. Not after he'd set her straight this last time. José had filed for and gotten sole custody of Cindy. With no baby to play Mommy with, and no man dancing attendance, Sharon had tried to get Sebastian to take her back. But he'd finally managed to ignore the sweetly teary eyes and trembling smile that she could dredge up at will. They didn't work on him anymore.

"I'll go on home now. I'll be back around midnight to check on you. Good night, Sebastian." She started to leave, then turned back to the cat who'd curled up next to the bed. "Good night, cat. Have you named him, by the way? You can't continue to call him 'cat' all the time."

"Why not?"

"I don't know." She smiled. "I guess you can, if you want."

"If you left it to me, I'd call him the Terminator."

"Terminator! Why?"

"Seems appropriate, what with trying to bean

me on the head with a shingle and scare me to death with that mouse. What would you call him?"

"Me? I don't know. I'm fond of myths and legends." When Sebastian rolled his eyes, she smiled. "And you know how I feel about magic. I think I'd call him Merlin. Merlin, the magical cat."

"Merlin, the Terminator."

"If you say so." Danni's smile became a grin. "I'll be back in a while."

Sebastian grinned back. "I'll be waiting."

He continued to grin long after she'd left. He'd smiled more the past few days than during the last eight years. And it was all because of Danni.

She wasn't his type at all. He'd always liked women who were tall and slender and practical. Sharon had been the one exception, and that was because she could assume a practical air when it suited her. Danni, on the other hand, was petite and curvy and as far from practical as you could get. So why did he dream about her? Why did he fantasize about *her* legs wrapped around him and *her* breasts crushed against him?

How was it that this particular woman could send his libido spiraling through the ceiling? He wished he knew. He'd love to be able to get his life back on a nice, predictable level—something it hadn't been since the day he met Danielle Sullivan.

Why did his room suddenly seem so plain? He got out of bed and began looking through a stack of pictures he'd propped against the wall. Maybe if he hung a few, it would brighten up the place.

Damn, they were every bit as dull as the room.

Wait a minute. "These are perfectly good pictures," he muttered to the cat, and leaned them against the edge of the bed to study them. The cat calmly walked to one and began to sharpen its claws on the frame.

"Everybody's a critic." He shooed the cat away. "Go catch another mouse, or something, would ya? Just don't bring it to me."

He decided against hanging the pictures and opted for a shower and shave instead.

After his shower he dressed again in jeans and shirt and sat on the edge of the bed towel-drying his hair—carefully. He looked up just as Merlin came back into the room with another mouse dangling from his mouth. Bemused, Sebastian watched the cat jump up on the windowsill and release the mouse. The terrified rodent leapt out of the open window and dashed across the porch roof. The cat blinked enigmatically at Sebastian, then meowed once.

"I'll be damned!" The towel Sebastian had been holding slipped out of his fingers to the floor. "You *did* understand what I said, didn't you?"

The cat just yawned, lifted his hind leg, and began to nonchalantly clean his bottom.

"No. That's crazy. You couldn't possibly have understood what I said. You simply did what any red-blooded cat worth its kibble would do in a farmhouse that's filled with mice." Sebastian dropped to his knees in front of the cat and looked into the inscrutable green eye that Merlin turned his way. "Didn't you?"

Merlin yawned again, tucked his front feet beneath him, and closed his eyes.

"What are you doing out of bed?"

Sebastian jumped at the sound of Danni's voice, then turned and gracefully got to his feet. "Hello to you too. I took a shower. What are you doing here so soon? It's not even close to midnight."

"I couldn't study for worrying about you," she admitted, and sat next to him. "It's a shame, too, because of that quiz in lab. Anyway, I thought that if I came here, maybe I'd get more done." She glanced at him, then looked at the dozing cat. "I hope that's all right," she added hesitantly.

Sebastian's heart flip-flopped. People didn't worry about him. He was too capable and controlled. Yet here was an utterly appealing elfin creature by the name of Danielle who did. He reached over and grasped one of her hands in both of his. "I'm all right," he said softly. "Really. But if it will make you feel better to stay, you're welcome to."

Danni looked up at him and smiled, a small, almost shy smile. It was utterly sweet. He smiled back, then their gazes met and held and the smiles faded. He saw the same hungry awareness that coursed through him flare in her eyes, and he watched as her tongue nervously swiped her lip. Sebastian reached up a finger and followed the path her tongue had taken, wiping across her bottom lip, then circling around the top.

"This isn't a good idea," Danni murmured weakly.

"I know." He slid his hand around her neck and grasped her braid, pulling it forward over her shoulder. His gaze never left hers, as he lifted her braid, running the tip of it down one cheek, then the other, then around her mouth.

"You don't get involved with people you work with," she protested, her voice even weaker than before.

"That's right," he whispered. "I don't." He wrapped her rope of hair around his hand and ever-so-gently tugged her closer.

"And—and you said we—you said we should make sure this doesn't—doesn't happen again." Her eyelids fluttered, then closed, as their faces drew closer together.

"Yes," he whispered against her mouth. "It shouldn't." His lips moved over hers in the barest of kisses. He kissed one corner of her mouth, then the other. He nibbled at her top lip, then the bottom one. But his mouth never fully covered hers. This would be a good time to stop, he thought, before their lips actually met.

He pulled back with the intention of doing just that and found his gaze lingering on the smooth skin of her throat. It looked tender, soft, delectable. One taste. He had to have one taste. He moved his lips down to the hollow of her throat. Danni's head tilted back to allow him better access. Sebastian took full advantage of it, sucking delicately, nipping with his teeth, then soothing with his tongue. He left a moist trail up to her ear, where he took her lobe into his mouth and sucked on it.

"Sebastian?" It was a question, a plea, a command.

And he was lost. "Yes, Danni?"

He kissed her then, totally, completely, with a hot and urgent hunger that demanded to be fed. His tongue possessed her, conquered her.

And when her tongue echoed his demand, he became the conquered.

His hand clutched convulsively at her hair, then slid over her back, pressing her closer. The soft mounds of her breasts fit perfectly against the harder planes of his chest. She made a low sound in her throat.

"Do you want me to stop?" he groaned against her lips.

"No. Yes. I . . . yes."

Sebastian sucked in his breath and, with an iron will, slowly pulled away and released her, running his fingers down her arms as he did so.

"Sebastian—" Her voice was full of frustration, confusion.

"Danielle, what are we doing?"

"I don't know." She brushed her hair back with a shaky hand, then moved to the chair. "I—it might be best if you, if we—you know."

"Yeah." Sebastian chuckled dryly. "We're batting a thousand, aren't we?"

"At what? Not getting involved?"

"Yeah."

"Maybe we are." She took a deep breath and brushed strands of hair away from her face. "Apparently, neither of us wants emotional involvement. I've got too many things to do before I settle down." She cocked her head. "Why don't you want to get involved?"

"I was married once. It didn't work out. So I've decided no more involvements, no more emotional garbage that passes for love."

Danni nodded. "I can understand that." She fell silent, her eyes narrowed in thought. "Tell me, do you have any objections to a no-strings-attached kind of thing?"

"What are you suggesting?" His gaze lingered on her still-swollen rosy lips.

She turned her head from him, looking at the cat, who still sat on the windowsill. "Well, I find you very attractive, and I can't help but think about what it would be like if you—if we, you know, had an, um, affair." She turned her gaze back to Sebastian.

He couldn't have been more stunned had she sprouted fairy wings and started to fly. She was watching him carefully now, and he tried to keep his expression blank. But a sudden vision of the two of them entwined in this bed burned itself into his mind. He could see it as clearly as if it had already happened. Her sun-blond hair would be spread over the pillow, her eyes glazed with desire. He could almost feel her silky-skinned breasts pressed against his chest, her slim legs wrapped around him, their bodies moving together in passion.

He felt his body react to the thought, but

Danni was too busy studying his face to notice. "Have an affair?" Thank God his voice didn't squeak.

"I don't know. Maybe. Maybe not. Certainly not yet, but if we acknowledge the desire is there—you do find me attractive, don't you? I don't want to assume, but I mean, you keep kissing me, and so I figured—"

"I find you attractive," he said shortly.

"Well then, if we acknowledge the desire is there and that an affair *could* happen, but that we wouldn't have to get emotionally involved, then that would simplify things a great deal. We wouldn't have to do all this denying and tiptoeing around. See?"

"Yeah." He wasn't sure he saw at all. "Isn't this rather a cool, uh, businesslike way to make a decision like this?"

"And what's wrong with that? If more decisions were made like this, we'd all be better off. Anyway, we're not actually deciding to have an affair. We're just acknowledging that an involvement wouldn't have to tie either of us down. All we have to do is remember the rules. Rule number one is: Don't mistake passion for love. Rule number two is: Don't forget rule one."

"What about love?"

"What about it?"

"Don't you believe in love? You believe in

magic. Isn't love part and parcel of all that? Isn't love the fairy-tale ending?"

"Oh, yes, I believe in love. Love *is* magic, you know. But I don't have time for it now. Besides, it usually leads to marriage, and this isn't the time and certainly not the place for me to get married. There's a whole world out there I want to see, and hundreds, thousands, of things I want to do. Anyway, I certainly haven't fallen head over heels in love. Yet." She stopped and eyed him curiously. "You haven't fallen in love with me or anything, have you?"

"Oh, no. No, certainly not."

"Love and sex aren't the same thing, and as long as we remember that, this could work out quite well. An affair, if we decide at some future time to go for it, could be a pleasant interlude in both our lives."

Pleasant interlude, indeed! This was the strangest conversation he'd had in a long time. "I'm confused here. Are you suggesting we should just—just do it?"

"Of course not. Not right now, anyway. It may not even happen at all. I'm only saying that if we realize it could happen and keep in mind we're two full-grown adults with control over our own emotions, then we could go to bed without any deeper involvement."

"Just like that?"

"Just like that." Danni bent over and unzipped her book bag, dragging out a handful of notes. "Is it all right if I study here?"

"Huh? Oh, yeah. Sure." He watched in amazement as she began to study the papers in her hand. He felt peeved that she could apparently chat about making love one minute, then easily turn her attention to something totally different without missing a step. He, on the other hand, was still caught up in the mental images of the two of them loving each other passionately.

A pleasant interlude, huh? Not if he had anything to say about it. If—when—he made love to Danielle Sullivan, he wanted her to crave it. It wasn't pleasant he wanted. He wanted terrific, fantastic, earth-shattering. And he had a feeling he could have it with her. Only she had be to more than mildly interested. She had to burn.

Still, it was the most intriguing conversation he'd ever had. And it didn't surprise him in the least that he'd had it with her. After all, she was the most intriguing woman he'd ever met.

Did he buy it? Did I overplay it? No, I think I did an admirable job of playing it cool. And I don't think he suspected at all that I wasn't half as unruffled as I sounded. Maybe he won't even suspect that I have as much experience in my whole life as he probably gets on an ordinary Friday night.

Danni set down her notes and unashamedly studied Sebastian as he slept. She'd had to do something. If they had continued that infernal fencing with each other, working together would have become intolerable. And she wanted to work with him. Badly.

Besides, if the mutual desire between them had remained unacknowledged, it would have merely simmered beneath the surface until it fooled one or the other of them into thinking it was something more than simple chemistry. Okay, not-so-simple chemistry, but chemistry nonetheless.

Sebastian stirred and turned to one side, draping his arm over the cat, who slept cuddled beside him. The cat opened one sleepy eye, mewed slightly, then went back to sleep. Danni felt a warm tugging inside. She loved watching him sleep—she didn't know why.

He had such thick dark hair, with a finger-tickling wave to it. She had a feeling that if he allowed it to grow a little, it would curl even more. The silky curls sprinkled across his chest were the same rich walnut-brown color. She reached out a finger to touch them, then drew back her hand.

She had to behave herself, so she crossed her arms and shifted position in the chair, getting more comfortable. She loved watching him. She could watch him all night. With a deep sigh she allowed her heavy eyelids to close. For just a minute.

Danni swatted at the butterfly brushing her nose. It flew away, only to light on her cheek. "Go 'way," she mumbled and swatted at it again, only to have it light on her other cheek. With that, she forced open her eyes to find Sebastian sitting on the end of the bed with a feather in his hand.

"Good morning," he said, in his wonderfully soft, husky voice.

Danni, who'd slept lounging in the chair, sat bolt upright, wincing as several muscles moaned in protest at the uncomfortable positions they'd been forced into all night. "Good morning. How's your head?"

"Never better. Thanks for staying with me."

"I was glad to do it."

"What time do you have to be at your lab?"

"Omigosh! What time is it?"

"About eight."

"Drat. I have to be there at nine o'clock, and it'll take me forty minutes to get to Norfolk. I haven't had a shower and—oh, I fell asleep before I even had a chance to finish studying. I'm going to flunk that quiz. I know it!"

"What subject?"

"Animal physiology." Danni was stuffing her papers back into her book bag as she answered.

"How long is your lab going to take?"

Danni stood, hoisting the overloaded bag over one shoulder. "A couple of hours, then I need to go to the library. I've got to run. Maybe I'll have time to change my T-shirt and brush my hair, anyway."

"Why don't I drive you and you can study on the way?"

Danni stopped in her tracks. "Drive me?"

"I need to pick up a few more things in Norfolk anyway, and I'm sure I can find something to do to kill time until around one."

Danni smiled, her eyes luminous as she looked at him. "Thank you. Thank you so much. Maybe we can go to lunch while we're there. My treat."

"My treat."

"Nonsense. I owe you for the favor."

"I was going into Norfolk anyway."

"At least let me reimburse you for the gas."

"Danni, don't argue. Go change your clothes. I'll be at your house in twenty minutes."

"Yoo-hoo." At the tap on the window Sebastian looked up to see Danni. He got out of the car and opened the trunk so she could put away her book bag. "How'd you do on the quiz?"

Danni didn't answer. Instead, she stared over his shoulder with a look of amused surprise on her face. "Who's your friend this time?"

Sebastian glanced around and saw a pigeon sitting on the roof of his car about a foot from his shoulder. "I don't know. Maybe it's one of Merlin's friends."

"More like Merlin's dinner."

"I don't know about that. Merlin's caught two mice, that I've seen, and he's let both go unharmed."

"Maybe he's softhearted."

"Softheaded, more likely."

"Well, this bird certainly seems to have taken a shine to you." They both watched as the little gray pigeon bobbed a step closer, then another. "Go ahead. Stick out your hand."

"And do what?"

"See if he'll let you touch him."

"That's ridiculous," he said, even as he slowly reached out. "Pigeons often look for a free handout, but they don't usually let strangers touch . . ." He ran his fingers lightly over the bird's head. "I'll be damned."

Then they both stared in amazement as another pigeon landed beside the first, just as close, and stood neck outstretched, as if waiting to be petted as well. Danni gave Sebastian a curious look. "Have you always drawn animals like this?"

He slowly shook his head. "No. But there's a perfectly logical explanation. We're next to the campus. The pigeons are probably used to getting fed. That's all." When he saw Danni's skeptical look, he added more forcefully, "That's all!"

"But, Sebastian, doesn't it seem odd? I mean, between Merlin the cat and Jonathan Livingston Pigeon here . . ." Her words trailed off at Sebastian's muffled curse, so she simply smiled and led the way into the café.

They chatted casually as they ate cheeseburgers and curly fries. Sebastian would peer over Danni's shoulder out the window at the two pigeons still perched on top of his car, then he'd meet Danni's eyes, and they'd twinkle at him. Nothing in his life made sense. Not since Danni Sullivan fluttered into it.

"So what are we going to do this afternoon?" Danni asked, as she swiped the last fry in catsup.

"I expect to go back to town and find out if they ever intend to install my telephone."

"Oh, Jamie and Buford will get around to it. They operate on a different timetable than the rest of the world."

"I don't care what their timetable is. When I talked to them Wednesday, they promised to have my phone hooked up by Thursday, and it's now Friday and still no phone."

Danni sighed. "They didn't specify Thursday of what week, did they?"

"No, but—"

"You need to pin them down a little more specifically. If they said they'd have it in by Thursday, they'll have it in by Thursday—of some month." At Sebastian's exasperated expression, she grinned. "Hey, you wanted small-town life, you got small-town life."

She studied him as he ate the last of his burger. He was so cute when he was baffled or miffed or exasperated. More chinks in his armor. And she had a feeling that the man inside the armor was going to be something to behold. She shook her head and surged to her feet, tugging her purse strap up over her arm. "I guess we should go."

By the time they got out to the car, another pigeon had joined the first two. "I wonder if someone's doing a remake of *The Birds*," quipped Danni, snapping her mouth shut at Sebastian's look.

"Very funny," he muttered, and bent slightly to unlock his car door. This put him eye-to-eye with the first pigeon, which bobbed a step closer and cooed at him. "For Pete's sake, would you leave me alone?" As if of one mind, the three birds took to the air. Sebastian dropped his keys.

He bent down to pick them up, then stood to meet Danni's wide-eyed stare. "Don't say a word," he warned. "Don't say a word."

Danni held up her hands. "I wouldn't dream of it. Actions speak louder, anyway."

She hung around most of the afternoon, while he waited for Jamie and Buford, who'd promised to show up "today, Doc. Keep yer shirt on." He dealt with the steady trickle of business, including a house—well, a farm—call to check on a milk cow off her feed.

Danni polished the old maple cabinets in the main examining room, hung curtains in the waiting room, and finished setting up cages in the back room. Sebastian, who between the occasional patient spent most of the afternoon organizing his supplies so they'd be easier to find, watched her flit around.

He'd always been a bit of a loner and disliked having people underfoot. But he loved having Danni around. She certainly wasn't quiet though. She hummed to herself in the examining room, sang out loud in the waiting room, and whistled off-key in the back.

He still wasn't sure why he was so drawn to Danni since she wasn't at all his type. But attracted to her he was.

Maybe what Danni had said last night was right on the money. If they acknowledged their attraction and accepted it, they'd be better off. Sweet, hot passion and no commitments. And maybe, just maybe, he'd get her out from under his skin.

FIVE

"Well, I think we're about ready."

Sebastian's head jerked around. "Ready for what?" Did she know what he'd been thinking?

"Ready to actually take in animals overnight. What did you think I meant?"

"I—nothing." She didn't know. He was almost disappointed. "You've been a big help today. Thank you."

"Are you ready to make the rounds tomorrow?"

"Uh, yes. Do you have a list of where to go?"

"As a matter of fact, I have it in my purse." She paused and looked around. "Wherever my purse is. I could've sworn I put it in the corner in the waiting room." They proceeded to spend the next fifteen minutes looking for the misplaced purse, finally locating it inside one of the cages in the back.

In triumph, Danni snared it and held it high. "I've got it. How did it wind up in there? And what did I want it for?"

"The list?"

"Oh, right." She stopped and dug through the oversized purse.

Sebastian's mouth fell open at what she had in there. She'd have been a hit on *Let's Make a Deal*. If game-show host Monty Hall had asked for someone with a lemon, a pair of pink socks, a romance novel, a box of crayons, and a television remote control, she'd have won the prize. "Here it is," she exclaimed, and waved a piece of paper. "Let's see. Mrs. Walling has asked that you come by to meet Peanut. It's almost time for his weekly baths to start up for the summer, and she wants him to get used to you. Then, old man Petrie is concerned about his mare. She's been favoring one of her front legs. John McLendon has a mare breeding for the first time, and he needs to have you check her out. And Magda would like you to come back out to her place. She's adopted five more cats from the animal shelter over in the next town."

"Five more?"

"She has an arrangement with the shelter that if they hold on to cats more than two weeks and can't adopt them out, she takes them. Usually, she manages to find them a home, but if she can't, well, they stay with her."

Sebastian shrugged. He couldn't fault her for that. "Did Dr. Adams ever make some sort of arrangement with her—a payment schedule or discount or anything?"

"No. I don't think it ever occurred to him. Besides, up until a few months ago, she only had about a dozen or so cats."

"Well, that's something I'll discuss with her. Maybe a quantity discount."

A smile lit Danni's eyes, and her face softened. She laid her hand on his arm. "That's a wonderful thing to do. You are a very special man, Sebastian Kent."

Sebastian looked first at her violet-blue eyes, glowing with soft silver lights, then down at her delicate hand resting on his arm. He had the peculiar feeling that all his thoughts about hot sex and no encumbrances had been ridiculous.

So why couldn't he stop? he asked himself even as he lifted her hand to his lips. He brushed his mouth across the backs of her fingers, then turned her hand over and pressed a kiss in the middle of her palm. He heard her breath catch, and his gaze met hers. He saw in her eyes all the breathless awareness he could have wished for.

Keeping her hand in his, he pulled her closer. He reached out his other hand and cupped her face, tilting it up to his. "Danielle?" he whispered.

"I know."

He didn't kiss her right away. He traced his thumb around her lips while he tried to tell himself he was crazy. It was sheer madness to want her like this, sheer insanity to need to taste her lips again. He lowered his mouth to hers. Okay, so he was insane.

And if he wasn't already mad for wanting her, the feel of her lips would have driven him mad. He tried to convince himself that her lips weren't the softest he'd ever kissed or the sweetest. He tried. But he failed.

And he tried to tell his arms that they would have felt the same wrapped around any woman. But they didn't believe him. . . .

When she parted her lips beneath his and invited him inside, his heart slammed against his chest. And when her hands splayed over his back holding him closer, he felt a trembling begin deep within. It was the shaking of the very foundations of everything he had believed for the last four years. He believed he didn't want another relationship, but he began to see otherwise. And he especially didn't want to get involved with another butterfly. But somehow he was captivated by the one perched on his hand.

But butterflies needed room to fly. Reluctantly, he gentled, then stilled, his lips on Danni's.

The soft, unfocused look in her eyes was almost his undoing. He wanted nothing more than to crush her lips beneath his again. And because he wanted it so much, he decided it would be safest—and sanest—not to. At least not until he figured how to hold a butterfly and let it fly free at the same time.

"Sebastian?" Danni's voice was the barest whisper.

Sebastian couldn't help brushing his hand down her cheek. "Thanks for all your help today, Danielle. What time do you want me to pick you up tomorrow?" His voice was warm and gentle but held an unmistakable tone of dismissal.

Danni took a deep breath. "Um, whatever time you want to get started is okay with me. I work for you, remember?"

Sebastian smiled. He wondered how long she'd remember that fact. "I'll pick you up at ten then." He walked her to the front door. "By the way, do you want to take some food home? I'll never be able to use up all they've brought."

Danni followed him into the kitchen. "How about if I take a platter of fried chicken off your hands?" Her voice still held a trace of the shakiness of a few minutes before.

Sebastian tried to ignore it and opened the stuffed refrigerator and handed her a platter wrapped in aluminum foil. "Sure you won't take two? I must have the equivalent of a coop of chickens. And I'd be delighted to throw in a casserole or two. Would you like broccoli? I have four different ones, all with cheese on top, and I have at least that many corn puddings." He handed her one of each.

He piled one of several plates of biscuits on top of everything else and grabbed one of the seven pies on the kitchen counter. He opened the front door to help her put everything in her car, and they both stopped dead. There, on the porch railing, sat two pigeons.

Danni's eyes widened, and she pursed her lips a moment, then said, "Well, if it isn't Jonathan Livingston Pigeon and friend."

"They're not the same ones." Sebastian shook his head and murmured, more to himself than her, "It can't be."

"Yes, it could be." She cast a sidelong glance at him. "It depends on what you're willing to believe."

"I believe what's logical and probable."

"Sebastian, when are you going to learn that being logical all the time is boring? And some things defy logic." She paused, pursed her lips, and continued, "You know, the way I see it, it's either that cat or the knock on your head."

"What is?"

"Well, you said you'd never had this effect on animals before, but since Merlin showed up, and you got bonked with the shingle, things have gotten positively spooky, don't you think? I wonder if it could be magic?"

Her voice was dead serious, but she had those same aggravating sparkles in her eyes. Humor and whimsy? Or was she serious?

Sebastian spent the evening staring at the television and eating Oreo cookies, but he couldn't have told anyone what he watched. His mind was busy examining and sorting facts.

Fact one: A six-toed odd-eyed cat was interesting, certainly, but not extraordinary. So what did that mean? Nothing.

Fact two: He told the cat to go catch a mouse, and it brought him a mouse. Big deal. His old farmhouse was full of mice, so that meant nothing.

Fact three: Two pigeons sat on the roof of his car. They were near the school campus and were probably used to handouts. Meaning? Nothing.

Fact four: Two pigeons that looked like the first two showed up on his porch railing. Pigeons looked like pigeons. And if he thought it meant anything, then he'd been spending too much time with Danielle and not enough with average sensible people. Ah, he thought with satisfaction, logic would win out every time!

Still, as he was getting ready to turn out the light, he couldn't resist asking the cat, who was dozing on the windowsill, if he'd like to sleep on the bed instead. And he chose to ignore the sense of relief he felt when the cat simply opened one sleepy eye and closed it again. Smiling to himself, Sebastian turned over and went to sleep.

When he awoke the next morning, his cheek was nestled against something warm and soft. For a split second he imagined it was Danni's full breast. He couldn't help but take the fantasy one step further. He'd move his cheek from her breast and take her tight nipple in his mouth, making her catch her breath and clutch at his head. Then he'd slide his hands down her body to her silky nest of curls—they'd have to be a delicate blond—and pleasure her until she pleaded with him to take her.

He liked the idea of her pleading with him to take her. He liked it so much that he felt himself swell and throb with need. Sebastian sighed in frustration and tried to will himself back into that pleasant twilight that fell between sleeping and wakefulness. He snuggled his cheek back into the softness next to it, then heard a strange rumbling begin beneath his ear. He opened his eyes and lifted his head to see the cat curled up on his pillow. That was all he needed, Sebastian thought, to wake up every morning with a mouth full of fur.

"Why don't you go back and sleep on the windowsill?" he muttered, then stopped dead as the cat raised his head with a regal air and sniffed as if to remind Sebastian that *he* had invited him to sleep on the bed. Not that Sebastian needed reminding.

Okay, he told himself, fact five: The cat slept on the bed. Cats loved comfort. The bed was comfortable. So this also meant nothing. Nonetheless, as Sebastian swung his feet to the floor, he felt a pounding begin in his head. All this nonsense was giving him a headache.

He popped a couple of headache tablets with his coffee as he ate cold fried chicken for breakfast and read the town's weekly paper. He felt distinctly better after that. *The White Creek Gazette* was a chatty little paper full of small-town news. It was a pleasant and very welcome change from the recitations of robberies, murders, and political maneuverings he was accustomed to reading in the morning.

He enjoyed reading about the town-beautification fund drive headed by Danielle Sullivan, an accounting of a baseball game between the volunteer fire department and the church choir (winning run by Danielle Sullivan, who slid into home plate headfirst), an article about the out-of-town guests staying with the Fosters. There was even a welcome to Dr. Sebastian Kent, the new vet from the Big Apple.

For a lady who insists that she's leaving town as soon as she gets her degree, she sure is head-over-heels involved in activities around here. Sebastian wondered if she knew that every town-council meeting she attended, every baseball game she played in, every committee she headed, was one more giant taproot anchoring her to this place.

He knew about taproots. He'd avoided putting them down in New York. Even when he'd married Sharon, he'd looked for an apartment, not a house. He'd looked for an office to lease, not buy. Maybe subconsciously he'd realized that Sharon would never be anything but temporary. But here, now that was another story. He'd only been in town a short time, and he already loved it.

He loved the overt friendliness of the people—even if they didn't get your phone installed on time. He liked the sound of crickets and whippoorwills outside his window, instead of the muffled hum or outright roar that went on night and day in the city. He liked being able to leave his door unlocked.

He liked the idea of getting to know nearly everyone in town by name, and stopping to chat about the weather with the postmistress when he went to mail a letter. He even liked knowing that in White Creek, Virgie Pace, who dressed like the grandma from hell, was a charming eccentric. Where he'd lived in New York, she probably wouldn't have rated a second glance.

He left the house about 9:55 and met Danni, who sat on her front porch swing, sipping a cup of tea. She looked charmingly sleepy-eyed when she yawned, then smiled up at him.

"I'm sorry," she apologized. "I've only been up a few minutes. I overslept this morning because I studied half the night."

She was dressed in faded jeans and a sleeveless red button-front shirt. No pink or purple? He was almost disappointed. Then she yawned again and stretched. The buttons pulled a little, and he saw a telltale bit of pink lace between. Oh, Lord. He doubted he'd be able to look at her the rest of the day without thinking about what she was wearing under that bright cherry-red shirt.

"I think we'd better go," he said abruptly. "Where to first?"

"I guess we should go by Mrs. Walling's first. She goes over to the church after lunch on Saturdays and makes sure everything's ready for Sunday. Speaking of Sunday, will you be going to church tomorrow? It would be a good place to begin getting to know people."

"I thought I might. What time are services?"

"Catholic mass is held there at eight A.M. Protestant Sunday school classes are at ten. Church services at eleven."

"Catholic mass?"

"The nearest Catholic church is about thirty minutes away. A few folks drive into Waverly or Norfolk, and a few want to stay here. Father Patrick stops by here on Sunday mornings on his way to ten o'clock mass in Suffolk. Gregory doesn't seem to mind."

"Who's Gregory?"

"The preacher. You'll like him, I think. He's young and energetic and full of passion and involved in a million causes. Half the women in church have a crush on him, and the other half are pushing their daughters at him." She chewed thoughtfully on the inside of her lip, then frowned. "Of course, that may change somewhat when they meet you."

She talked about this "Gregory" with real warmth in her voice. Already, Sebastian was sure he wasn't going to like him. *All* the women either had crushes on him or wanted to marry off daughters to him? Did Danni, too, have a crush on him? And if she did, what business did she have kissing Sebastian as she did?

"Now be careful of Peanut," Danni warned when they pulled into Mrs. Walling's driveway. "He doesn't take to strangers right away."

Sebastian didn't have to be told to be careful around a brahma bull—or any animal weighing in excess of a thousand pounds. He could see the huge head of the bull over the wooden fence that separated a small pasture from the Wallings' backyard. He walked over to the fence, staying six or seven feet back to allow the bull to smell his scent. Danni, on the other hand, hopped up on the fence and scratched the bull between his capped horns.

To Sebastian's surprise, the bull stretched out his head in his direction and made a lowing sound.

Danni raised an eyebrow. "Well, isn't that strange?"

"What?"

"I think he wants you to pet him."

Sebastian eyed the bull cautiously. "How can you tell?"

"He asked you to, just as clear as day. He stuck his nose out in your direction and mooed."

Sebastian took a couple of steps closer and held out his hand, ready to jump back if necessary. Peanut butted his head against the palm of his hand like a dog wanting a pat. Sebastian scratched the bull behind the ear and turned to Danni.

"I don't believe it," Danni murmured. "It usually takes him several hours, even days, to get used to a person. Honest." She stared a moment longer, then exhaled a deep breath. "One more spooky thing."

"Don't even start, Danielle. I'm a vet, and I'm comfortable around animals. Obviously, he can tell."

"Right," Danni said. "But he couldn't tell Dr. Adams was a vet, because he chased him halfway across the pasture the first time he came out here."

They stayed a few more minutes and chatted with Mrs. Walling, then left for John McLendon's. John had a spread just outside of town where he raised a few horses, one of which was breeding for the first time. Everything was fine, and after eating the lunch Mary McLendon served in her large, cheery kitchen, they headed back to Magda's.

Magda wasn't home, but she'd left a note tacked to her front door telling them the cats were inside in her utility room. Sebastian took care of the cats, then left his bill taped to the utility-room door. Danni whistled when she saw the amount. That wasn't just a little discount he was giving Magda. He was charging her only a few cents over cost. Well, damn. How was she supposed to keep a safe, uncommitted distance when he kept doing these impossibly sweet things? How could she hope to have a terrific passionate affair without real emotional involvement when she liked every single thing she learned about him?

Not that she was falling in love with him, she assured herself. Maybe they could become best friends. She wondered if it were possible to have a flaming affair with one's best friend without damaging the friendship.

"Where's this Mr. Petrie live?"

"Oh, he lives farther down this road. I'm sorry, Sebastian, I should have suggested we bring my Jeep again. This is going to play hell with your transmission. Not to mention your front-end alignment."

"The road into Magda's wasn't so bad. I only hit a half-dozen potholes."

"Sebastian, Magda had the road bulldozed out between her house and the main road about three weeks ago."

Sebastian paused as this sank in. "You mean from here on it gets worse?"

Danni nodded. "Unfortunately."

His forehead creased, he stared at the road ahead as if searching for obstacles. Finally, he said, though with a tone of uncertainty in his voice, "My car can make it. It's lived through two years of New York traffic. I'm sure it'll be . . . just fine."

Danni winced every time Sebastian's sturdy Volvo hit a pothole. And he hit plenty. He kept his muffled curses to a minimum, mostly because he never unclenched his teeth. Poor thing, Danni thought, as the pained look on his face deepened with every yard they traveled.

"I swear I'm going to go into Norfolk and trade this thing in on a pickup truck."

"That might be best," Danni murmured.

"How much farther is it?"

"About a quarter of a mile."

"Thank God."

Danni grinned sympathetically at his heartfelt exclamation. "I traded in a cute little red Mazda for my Jeep last year. All it took was one trip out to Petrie's, and I know I left parts of my engine in at least four different potholes. And you can't even imagine what this road is like after a heavy rain."

"I have a good imagination. That picture boggles the mind. I definitely need a pickup. Is this it?" Sebastian eyed a structure that looked as if a million nails and ten coats of paint wouldn't help it. It would still look as if a strong sneeze would blow it over.

"This is the place. Petrie calls it Ferndale. He thinks a fancy name will give it some class. He doesn't realize that this place could take a bath in class and still look like a junk heap. He's extremely proud of it, though, so be complimentary."

Sebastian held up a hand as if taking a solemn vow. "I promise."

"Sally and Pepper are out in the barn. Sal's the one who's limping. You won't have any trouble telling which is which. Pepper is a gelding. I'll let Petrie know you're here." Danni headed toward the dilapidated front door.

Sebastian watched as Danni walked away. He really did like the way she walked. She walked with an unhurried yet purposeful stride. It was a boyishly free stride, but with that tempting feminine sway to her hips that he'd noticed before. And great hips they were. Were those tempting hips wearing purple panties? Or pink ones to match the lacy whatever-it-was under her shirt?

He reluctantly turned away and went to the barn. Sally was a pretty chocolate-brown mare with a white blaze and two white feet. As soon as the horse saw Sebastian, she hung her head over the door and nickered softly. He gently rubbed her nose and murmured to her.

When he felt reasonably sure she was comfortable with him, he went into the stall with her and ran gentle, searching fingers down each leg. "Now which leg is it that's hurting you, girl?"

To his amazement, she lifted her right front leg. Sebastian heard a noise behind him and looked over his shoulder to see Danni standing there with a strange expression on her face.

"You *can* talk with animals," she murmured. "This really is magic."

Sebastian sighed. "Don't start. This might not even be the leg." But his seeking fingers and quick eyes discovered an abscess in the right hoof.

"You were saying?" Danni asked smugly.

Fact six. "If the foot is sore, the mare wouldn't be putting a lot of weight on it anyway," he said, as he prepared to drain the abscess.

"Don't be so quick to disparage magic, Sebastian. You have to admit things are getting downright weird."

Sebastian ignored that. "Where's Mr. Petrie?"

"He'll be here in a few minutes. He's out in his garden. I have a feeling you're going to get paid in produce."

Sebastian shrugged. "Fresh vegetables might be a nice change from fried chicken and assorted casseroles. I may never want to see another vegetable with cream sauce or cheese on it. Can you get me a bucket of hot water? And see if Mr. Petrie has any Epsom salts."

Danni was back in a few minutes with Mr. Petrie and the supplies. "Sebastian? This is Lemuel Petrie." She indicated a tall, lean, grizzled man who looked to be somewhere between fifty and a hundred and ten. "And this is Dr. Kent."

Sebastian shook the man's callused hand. "Nice to meet you, Mr. Petrie."

"Folks around here jus' call me Lem. What'sa matter with ol' Sal here?"

"Nothing major. An abscess on the right front hoof. I've drained it and cleaned it. What you'll need to do is soak the foot every day in hot water and Epsom salts. Otherwise, keep it wrapped and dry for about a week. That'll take care of it."

"Guess I can't let her play in the back field then. Marshy ground, and she likes to go back there and nibble on the new grass."

"I'm afraid it's standing around on the wet ground that can cause this."

Petrie nodded. "I'll take care of it. I've got a bushel basket of stuff by your car. Hope that's all right."

"It'll be fine, I'm sure."

"The ladies from church have been by," Danni said. "And you know what that means. Sebastian's looking forward to some fresh vegetables for a change."

Petrie's weathered old face split into a wide grin. "Bet you're about fried-chickened out, ain't ya?"

"That's the truth."

"Well, I got a few peas in there, some lettuce, spinach, radishes, and a couple of heads of cabbage."

"That sounds great, thanks."

They talked a few minutes more, mostly about the erratic spring weather, then Sebastian and Danni left. They were silent on the all-too-bumpy ride back to the main road. Finally, Danni broke the silence. "Sebastian, I know you don't want to talk about it, but you have to admit that it does seem as if you can communicate with animals in some way."

"It's all been nothing but coincidence. There has been a sensible explanation for everything that has happened."

"Sebastian—"

"Danni, don't go on about magic and such. I mean, look at what you're suggesting—that I can actually talk to the animals, for heaven's sake!"

"Is that really so crazy?"

"Crazy? Yeah, it's crazy."

"There are a lot of things in this world we don't understand and can't explain. That doesn't make them any less real. Can you explain a rainbow?"

"There *is* a scientific explanation."

"There are—"

"Haven't we already had this discussion? I don't believe in magic. Period."

"But you should. There's a lot of magic in life. If you automatically disbelieve the unexplainable, you limit your horizons."

"So I'm supposed to believe that I can communicate with horses, cats, and pigeons?"

"Suppose, for a minute, that you could. Wouldn't it be marvelous? You're a vet. Haven't you ever entertained the thought?"

"It would certainly simplify things, all right, but simply because it would be nice to be able to do something doesn't mean we can."

"But, Sebastian, don't you believe in anything unexplainable?"

"Yeah. It'll always rain on the Fourth of July and, even in Alaska, it won't snow on Christmas Eve. Everything else has a logical explanation, even if we don't know what it is."

"And the logical explanation for what happened with Lem's mare?"

"Her foot was sore. She wouldn't be putting a lot of weight on it, anyway. It was only a coincidence that she happened to pick it up when I asked which leg it was. It was just a coincidence. Got it?"

"Tell me, Sebastian. Have you convinced yourself of that yet?"

SIX

"You're not facing up to reality."

"Reality? You call believing that someone can talk to animals reality? *You're* the one not facing reality, Danni. There's no such thing as magic."

"What would you call all the weird things that have happened?"

"Coincidence. Nothing but coincidence. Any reasonable person would be able to see that."

"But there have been too many coincidences. The cat, the pigeons, the horse—"

Sebastian slapped his palm against the steering wheel. "Dammit! I don't want to talk about this anymore, so drop it. Just drop it."

"Excu-u-use me. What's the matter? Am I hitting too close for comfort? You can't admit for even one minute that I might be right?"

Danni folded her arms and poked her chin out.

"You're not right," he said flatly.

"And you are?" Her voice rose a little. "Sebastian, life isn't always logical and orderly. Do you think that by pretending it is, you'll make it so?"

"At least I don't go around pretending I believe in leprechauns and unicorns!"

"Who says I'm pretending?" she snapped, turning her head toward the window. "Take me home."

"I was planning to."

That was the last either of them spoke until Sebastian pulled up in front of Danni's house. Her grandmother, dressed in blue jeans and a Hawaiian-print halter top, with her carrot-colored hair sticking out in every direction, waved at him, then went back to washing the pig that lounged in the child's swimming pool in the front yard. Sebastian rolled his eyes.

"Don't you say a word about my grandma!"

"I wasn't about to."

"I saw the look on your face."

"Looks aren't words."

"I know what you were thinking."

"And since when are thoughts against the law? Better yet, since when did you become psychic? How the hell do you know what I was thinking?"

"I just know, that's all. You're thinking my grandmother is odd."

"No odder than you!" he shouted.

Danni got out and slammed the car door hard. "Good-bye," she yelled, without turning around. She marched up her sidewalk, right past her grandmother, and went inside.

"Seems a bit miffed," Virgie Pace called out in a conversational tone.

Sebastian nodded and waved, then turned the car around and headed home. "Damn, stubborn, hardheaded, obstinate, flighty, stubborn"—hadn't he already said that?—"headstrong, capricious, opinionated, unreasonable . . ." He couldn't think of any more descriptives for Danni. Except maybe sexy, charming, generous, kind, and nuts.

What was there about her that got his back up and sent his hormones into overdrive? He wanted to grab her and shake some sense into her. He also wanted to grab her and kiss the sense right back out of her. He pulled up in front of his house and got out. Dammit, she made him crazy. That was all there was to it. A few more days of working with her, and they'd be coming to cart him off to a rubber room. And if they didn't, he'd voluntarily turn himself in.

He sat on his front step and tried to put his

thoughts in order. Fact one: She was a will-o'-the-wisp. So? He didn't have to marry her.

Fact two: She turned him on more than any other woman he'd ever met. So? He still didn't have to marry her.

Fact three: She'd even brought up that business about no strings herself. He could take her to bed and love her right out of his system—without feeling guilty. Once he'd had her, he'd probably have control over his hormones and be able to concentrate on all the reasons why she drove him crazy, instead of concentrating on all the reasons she drove him crazy with need. Right, and cats could fly. He thought about Merlin. To be safe, he wouldn't say that out loud.

What was there about her that made him as itchy as a dog with fleas? He glared at the cat, who jumped up on the porch railing and meowed. He'd left Merlin inside, and none of the windows was open, so he didn't know how he got out—or want to know.

Okay, he had an oddball cat. Who cared? He didn't know why Danni kept harping on that darn cat and the bump on Sebastian's head, as if they were somehow responsible for all the strange things that were happening. They didn't have anything to do with it. If any outside force had an influence on the confusion in his life, it was Danni. The way he saw it, pandemonium followed her around like a puppy.

Sebastian looked up in time to see the two pigeons join Merlin on the railing. He jumped to his feet and went back out to the car. Days like this called for a beer. Or a six-pack. Luckily, Bosco Wilson's Food Mart didn't close until six, and it was only five-thirty now.

He drove to the little store and parked his car in one of the half-dozen spaces in front. This was the first time he'd been in Bosco's, and he had to stop for a moment and appreciate the flavor of the place. It had every bit as much atmosphere as any New York deli he'd ever been in—except this was pure rural. Cans of machine oil took shelf space next to cans of green beans. Packages of guitar strings sat alongside packages of disposable diapers. Sweet pickles occupied end caps next to mustache wax.

Danni was right when she'd made that joking remark about running to Bosco Wilson's Food Mart to pick up an extra pair of eyes. He *did* carry almost everything else. Including the six-pack of beer and bag of Oreos that Sebastian was looking for. He didn't even have to pay for them. Bosco's wife, Elsie, gave them to Sebastian as a Welcome to White Creek present.

He was feeling so much better when he got home, he'd decided to put the beer in the fridge instead of drinking it. At least, he'd decided to do that until he saw the two pigeons on the porch railing—one on either side of the cat.

He definitely needed a few beers to put that picture into perspective. Maybe afterward, pigeons sitting side by side with a cat wouldn't seem so strange. And after enough beer, it might even seem normal.

It didn't take six beers. It only took five. He wasn't used to drinking much anyway, and five beers on a stomach filled with nothing except a half-package of cookies had Sebastian feeling no pain.

As a matter of fact, he wasn't feeling much of anything at all, he mused, as he stared at the cat eating a helping of cold broccoli casserole. He didn't know how the cat got back in the house; he hadn't let him in, but now it didn't bother him. The two pigeons still sitting on the porch railing didn't bother him either. He wasn't even angry at Danielle anymore.

Unfortunately, the only feelings that weren't temporarily anesthetized were the desire that burned through him and the hunger that ate at him. He felt another surge of anger at Danni, this time because she wouldn't stay out of his head.

Maybe he was bewitched. Suppose she wasn't a butterfly at all, but a witch? That would explain a lot of things—like why he thought she was the most beautiful woman he'd ever met and why he was so fascinated with what she wore underneath her pink-and-purple T-shirts. And it might even explain why her eyes did that peculiar sparkly number. He found himself wondering what those witching eyes looked like when she'd been made love to. Did they sparkle then too? Or did they glow?

He didn't want to fall for her. He didn't. But he'd about reached the end of his endurance. Sebastian dropped his head into his hands and mumbled, "I wish you'd march around in someone else's head and leave me alone."

"Sebastian?"

When he looked up to find Danni staring down at him with a concerned look on her face, he groaned. "Why don't you and John Philip Sousa go somewhere else?"

"Are you okay?"

"I'm fine. What're you doin' here?"

"I came back to, well, to apologize for our—our little argu—disagreement." She stopped as if just noticing the empty beer cans lined up in a neat row on the kitchen table. "What's with the beer cans?"

He gave her a baleful look. What did she think was with them? Did she think he'd been feeding beer to the cat? Maybe he'd get arrested for contributing to the delinquency of a feline.

"I'm gonna practice target shootin' after a while and wanted some empty cans to shoot at. So I felt it my duty to provide the cans. You'll notice I did the best thing for the environment and used all-aluminum." He stifled a yawn.

"Right," Danni murmured with amused sarcasm. "As if anyone in his right mind would let someone in your condition near a gun."

"What condition? I'm not pregnant, I'm only relaxed."

"Do you do this kind of thing very often?"

"Yeah, sure. I had a drink last year, I think. New Year's Eve. Half a glass of champagne. Don't care much for it, but beer's okay. 'Specially with pizza."

He sighed. "You have any pizza? I only have fried chicken, and beer jus' doesn't work with chicken. Only problem with beer is, it makes me sleepy." He yawned again. "I'm not sleepy now though."

Danni, who could drink any two-hundred-pound linebacker under the table and not feel tipsy, didn't drink much because she didn't like it. Her Southern Baptist upbringing might have something to do with it too.

Wasn't Sebastian cute, though? When he was sober and in cool control, he was attractive as well as being devastatingly sexy. Now, however, he was cuddly cute. His usually neat hair was

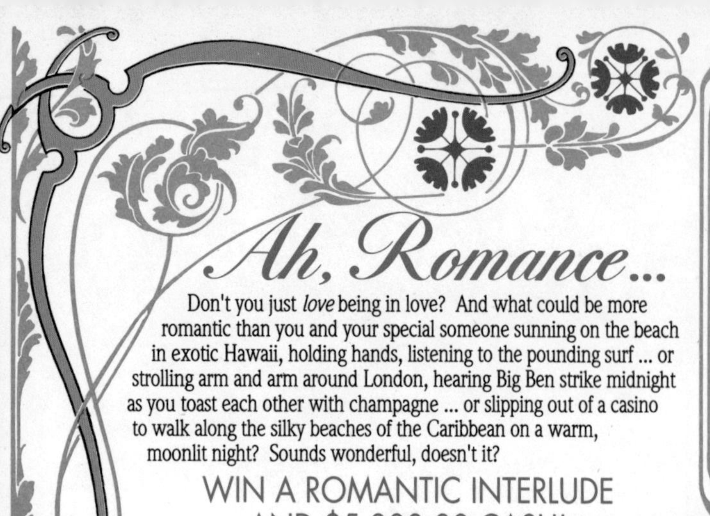

Don't you just *love* being in love? And what could be more romantic than you and your special someone sunning on the beach in exotic Hawaii, holding hands, listening to the pounding surf ... or strolling arm and arm around London, hearing Big Ben strike midnight as you toast each other with champagne ... or slipping out of a casino to walk along the silky beaches of the Caribbean on a warm, moonlit night? Sounds wonderful, doesn't it?

WIN A ROMANTIC INTERLUDE AND $5,000.00 CASH!

What's even *more* wonderful is that **you could win** one of these romantic **14-day vacations for two**, plus **$5,000.00 CASH**, in the Winners Classic Sweepstakes! To enter, just affix the vacation sticker of your choice to your Official Entry Form and drop it in the mail. It costs you nothing to enter (we even pay postage!) — so ***go for it!***

FREE GIFTS!

We've got **four FREE Loveswept Romances** and a **FREE Lighted Makeup Case** ready to send you, too!

If you affix the FREE GIFTS sticker to your Entry Form, four fabulous Loveswept Romances are yours absolutely FREE. Plus, about once a month, you'll get six *new* books hot off the presses, *before they're available in bookstores.* You'll always have 15 days to decide whether to keep any shipment, for our low regular price, currently just $13.50* — that's 6 books for the price of four! **You are never obligated to keep any shipment**, and may cancel at any time by writing "cancel" across our invoice and returning the shipment to us, at our expense. There's **no risk** and **no obligation** to buy, *ever.*

Now that's a pretty sweet offer, I think you'll agree — but we've made it even sweeter! We'll also send you the **Lighted Makeup Case** shown on the other side of this card — **absolutely FREE!** It has an elegant tortoise-shell finish, and comes with an assortment of brushes for eye shadow, blush and lip color. And the lighted mirror makes sure your look is always *perfect!*

BOTH GIFTS ARE ABSOLUTELY FREE AND ARE YOURS TO KEEP FOREVER, no matter what you decide about future shipments! So come on! You risk nothing at all — and you stand to gain a world of sizzling romance, exciting prizes ... and FREE GIFTS!

*(plus shipping & handling, and sales tax in NY and Canada)

ruffled and stuck out as though he'd run his hands through it a lot.

His normally sharp-sighted golden-brown eyes were heavy-lidded and drowsy. And his usually firm lips were curved in a silly grin. She grinned back. She couldn't help it. He looked like a shaggy teddy bear—a much-loved teddy bear who'd been washed one too many times. A teddy bear she wanted to take to bed and cuddle up with.

"Wanna split the last one with me?" He held it up with one hand, stifling yet another yawn with the other.

"I don't think you need another one," she said gently, taking the can from him.

"Then you can have the whole thing," he said with a magnanimous wave of his hand.

"Gee, thanks." She grimaced. "But I had left-over cold fried chicken for dinner, and like you said, beer just doesn't go with it. So why don't we put it into the refrigerator?"

"No room. Still full of cold fried chicken. I don't think I'm gonna ever eat any more chicken. Not broiled, boiled, or barbecued. But 'specially not fried." He squinted at her. "What're you smilin' at?"

"You're cute when you're tipsy."

"I'm not tipsy," he denied, and got to his feet. He grabbed the back of his chair. "The room's a little sideways."

Danni sighed good-naturedly and hooked her arm through his. "You're the one who's a little sideways, big guy."

"So you came to apologize, huh? That's nice. To admit you're wrong, I mean."

Danni raised an eyebrow. "I wasn't wrong."

"So why'd you apologize?"

"Because I'm sorry we argued. But I wasn't wrong. You were."

"I was not. There's no such thing as magic."

"You wanna explain the two pigeons still sitting on your front porch?"

Sebastian fell silent. "I've got a headache," he finally muttered.

Danni sighed. "Well, then, c'mon. Let's go upstairs."

"You gonna put me to bed—tuck me in and all that?"

"I guess I'd better. I can't leave you roaming the house in this condition."

"You can tuck yourself in with me."

Danni didn't say anything to that. But she drew in her breath at the thought. Except in her thoughts, *he* was tucking *her* in bed. He would scoop her up in his powerful arms and lay her gently on the bed, but only after jerking the covers away in one powerful tug. He'd say that he didn't want anything to come between them.

He would somehow magically smooth away her jeans and T-shirt, leaving her clad only in her favorite purple satin teddy. He would spread her hair over the pillow, then trail his hands over her shoulders to her breasts, down her sides to her hips, then down over her legs.

Then she'd get to touch him—his shoulders, his arms, his chest, his strong thighs. She wondered if his flat brown nipples were sensitive or the backs of his knees or the nape of his neck. She'd like to find out, she thought wistfully. Right now, though, she had a half-asleep sot on her hands.

As soon as his head hit his pillow, he smiled, yawned, muttered something about going to church in the morning, and went to sleep. Danni stood looking down at him. It occurred to her that for a man she'd known such a short time, she'd spent a lot of it tucking him in bed and watching him sleep. It was hard to believe she hadn't even known him a month. It seemed both as if she'd known him forever and hadn't known him nearly long enough.

Merlin jumped up next to Sebastian and got comfortable. She could hear his loud purr begin as she reached out and smoothed Sebastian's silky hair back from his forehead. A tender smile curved her lips as she bent down and pressed a kiss on his nose. She turned out the light and left.

The sun shone in the window with all the clarity and brilliance of an expertly cut diamond. It would be a good morning, thought Sebastian, if the elephants would stop stomping back and forth over his head. And if the ants would stop running around behind his itchy eyelids. And if the heavy weight lying across his chest would move. Suddenly, the weight on his chest *did* move, and Sebastian opened his eyes. He should have known. It was the damn cat.

He pushed the cat off with a groan and struggled to a sitting position. "You drove me to this," he muttered to Merlin, who jumped to the windowsill and began licking his paws. "You drove me to drink. You and the damned pigeons. And Danni. Let's not forget Danni."

He got to his feet and stumbled to a hot shower. "I'm a logical man, a sensible man," he said as he lathered up. "And she's already driven me nuts—even got me talking to myself."

He felt marginally better after his shower and a couple of headache tablets. He walked back into the bedroom wearing a towel around his waist and water droplets in the hair on his chest. He heard a gasp and an "Omigosh!" and turned around. "Hello, Danni," he said easily as he made sure the towel was secure. "Ever think about knocking first?"

"I did," she said lamely, forcing her gaze to the floor. "But you didn't answer."

"So you decided to walk right in."

She thought she detected amusement in his voice and looked up. He wasn't embarrassed by this at all, she realized. As a matter of fact, Danni could've sworn he was enjoying her discomfort if the laughter in his eyes was anything to go by. She rarely blushed but now felt the heat sweep up from her throat to her cheeks and again lowered her flustered gaze to the floor.

Her mouth felt dry, as if she'd been chewing talc. "I'll come back later."

"Leaving so soon? There had to be a reason you barged in, unless you were hoping to catch me *in* the shower, not just out of it."

Her face felt even hotter. "I wanted to see if you were going to church this morning. You, um, you mentioned something about it last night."

"Certainly." He added dryly, "I wouldn't miss meeting the pastoral heartthrob of White Creek. As a matter of fact, since it's after ten, I was going to get dressed pretty fast." He smiled wickedly and raised an eyebrow. "Do you want to watch?"

"I'll see you at church." Danni fled.

So this was the way to keep the upper

hand with Danni. Keep her off balance. For all her brave talk about no-strings relationships, Sebastian had the feeling she was really an old-fashioned small-town girl underneath. She even blushed, and he couldn't remember the last time he'd seen anyone do that. He was a sucker for women who could still blush.

He bent down to pull on briefs, then grimaced as more elephants stomped across his head. He'd better move a little more carefully—at least for the next few hours.

He arrived at church with a few minutes to spare. He had just enough time to find Danni and her grandmother and slide in next to them in the pew. He glanced at Danni and smiled, turned to watch the choir file in, then turned immediately back to Danni. She looked different. She wore a conservative pink suit, with lacy ruffles at the collar and cuffs. Her hair had been braided, then wound around her head in a surprisingly sophisticated coronet.

She looked almost conventional. Almost, but not quite. Those pink fairy earrings swung from her ears, pink ballet slippers adorned her feet, and the skirt of her suit looked as if it might be a little short when she stood up. He stared at the expanse of leg showing between the hem of her skirt and her knees. It might be a lot short.

The organist went into a rousing invocation,

and each and every chord reverberated in his head. He felt a little ill at ease sitting in church, not only because of the hangover, but also because he was lusting over the dainty blonde sitting next to him. Hung over and lusting—well, he was certainly in the right place.

The minister walked out to the pulpit, and Sebastian's eyes narrowed as he studied him. The Reverend Gregory Talbott *was* young, maybe thirty, with an unruly shock of red hair and a rebel's glint in his eyes. He certainly gave a terrific sermon, with passion and fire. Sebastian, who'd been prepared not to like him, found himself liking him anyway.

He changed his mind after the service, however, when the young minister gave Danni a big hug as they were leaving.

"Great play at the ball game last weekend. Can we count on you this week? We have a game Wednesday night."

"If you're going to be batting cleanup again, I'll be there. I'd hate to miss the sun glinting on your nice red angel's halo."

Gregory grinned. "When I was a kid, my father wasn't convinced this red hair was a halo—more like the fires of hell. How about you, Dr. Kent? Do you play baseball? We could always use another infielder. Most of our players tend to duck when a ball comes to them."

"I don't know what my schedule is going to be yet. But if I can make it, I'll let you know." He'd make it all right, to make sure Gregory didn't score any runs with Danni. No, Sebastian didn't like him at all, especially the way he kept a companionable arm around Danni's waist while he chatted with her grandmother.

Sebastian got hugs and handshakes from almost everyone who walked by him. He felt genuinely welcomed by the people in White Creek. He was invited to dinners, to afternoon socials, and weekend dances at the fire department. He smiled and greeted everyone who spoke to him, though he was hard-pressed to keep a sour gaze from lingering on Danni and Gregory.

When he turned to leave, Virgie Pace tapped him on the arm. He turned back to her with a forced smile, his gaze automatically sliding to Danni, who was still chatting with the minister.

"You will join us for Sunday dinner, won't you? Gregory will be there, too, and you'll get a chance to talk. You'll like him."

Why did everyone keep insisting he'd like the man? "I wouldn't miss it for the world. What time?"

"Any time. After all, an important part of Sunday dinner is to sit on the sofa and read the paper, while you wait for the roast to finish cooking. But if you'd like to change first, feel free. We don't stand on formality around here, and Greg and Danni usually manage to get down and dirty before the day is out anyway."

Sebastian snapped his head around. "What do you mean, 'down and dirty'?"

"They're both inveterate game players—Ping-Pong, croquet, badminton, checkers. Most every Sunday, they have something going."

Sebastian clenched his jaw so tight that it hurt. So this went on every Sunday? Just how close were they? He took some consolation that there was apparently no formal commitment between them. After all, not only did Danni not wear a ring, but she kissed Sebastian as if there were no tomorrow, and he didn't think she'd do that if she were committed to anyone else. She might be a butterfly, but he felt she was an honorable one.

He really wanted to dislike Gregory, but as the afternoon wore on, he found he couldn't. For starters, he drove a well-maintained classic Ford Mustang. And any man who could appreciate the virtues of a car Sebastian had always coveted couldn't be all bad. Next, the car was festooned with bumper stickers that proclaimed Greg's membership in a number of environmental organizations—several of which Sebastian belonged to.

What helped the most, however, was that Sebastian could see nothing more than simple friendly interest in the interaction between Danni and Greg. Even the game of croquet they were playing when Sebastian arrived showed only amiable competition.

Virgie Pace was dressed much differently than she'd been that morning at church. She was back to her biker look, dressed in heavily patched jeans, T-shirt, and black leather boots. "They make a nice-looking couple, don't they?" she asked Sebastian as she met him at the front door, her shrewd eyes never leaving his face.

He glanced out into the front yard where they were finishing up their game and tried not to squirm under Virgie's sharp-eyed scrutiny. He shrugged. "Why do you say that?"

"No reason. But I happen to prefer the way she looks with brunettes. Greg's a great-looking redhead, to be sure, but I always thought petite blondes looked better with tall brunettes, don't you?" She winked at him and handed him a glass of iced tea.

Sebastian wasn't sure he had any business admitting it, but he liked petite blondes—like Danni—better with tall brunettes—like him—better too. Greg came in, followed by Danni, flushed and laughing. With the color in her cheeks, little tendrils of hair escaping her braid, and the animation of her expression, she was indescribably lovely. This was the way she might look after making love, Sebastian thought, and felt a stab of desire so strong that he rearranged the newspaper over his lap, to be safe.

The way she'd looked this morning in her slightly too-short skirt was nothing compared to the way she looked now in too-short purple shorts and crop-top. Sebastian wasn't sure whether to look at the expanse of leg revealed by the shorts or the tempting bit of flesh revealed where the top of the shorts didn't quite meet the bottom of her shirt.

"Who won?" He could only thank God that his voice didn't croak.

"He did." Danni tossed her head, setting her braid to swinging back and forth. "But only because he cheats."

Greg shrugged and grinned. "Now would I cheat? I have it on the best authority that I have an honest face."

Danni punched him lightly on the shoulder. "What, did you bribe the board of deacons to say that?" She peeked around into the kitchen to see if her grandmother needed any help, then flopped next to Sebastian on the sofa and grabbed a section of the paper from him.

She took one look at it and said, "Yuck, I don't read the news. Do you have the travel section anywhere in there?" She tossed the news section to Greg, then began looking through the other papers in Sebastian's lap. Sebastian closed his fingers lightly around hers as if to still her hand and went through the stack of paper in his lap himself, then handed her the travel section.

Danni immediately began looking through the paper, though in her mind she wasn't seeing the ads for exotic locales, she was seeing only one thing—the way Sebastian had looked that morning wearing that devilish smile and a towel. She'd thought of little else since then.

She glanced over at Greg. Now he was an attractive man, a man that most of the females in the congregation drooled over. She could appreciate Greg's looks the way she could appreciate a work of art. He might very well look good wrapped in a towel, but for some reason the idea didn't stir her the way the idea of Sebastian did, and with Greg, she certainly didn't fantasize about removing the towel. She bit back a smile, wondering if it were at all sacrilegious even imagining a preacher in a towel.

But with Sebastian, she could imagine running her palms over the damp hair on his chest, smoothing away the moisture. Or maybe she'd run her lips over it, catching the droplets of water with her tongue. She'd run her fingers around the edge of the towel, then tug gently at it, pulling it loose. She'd drop it on the floor, then smooth her hands over his tight buttocks and—

"Danielle, would you mind taking the rolls out of the oven? I've got my hands full at the moment."

"What?" Danni looked up, confused. For a moment there she'd been in Sebastian's bedroom removing an obtrusive towel; now she was back in her living room clutching the travel section of the Sunday paper. What a disappointment! "I'll be right there, Gran." She took a quick peek at Sebastian and Greg, to see if they'd noticed her daydreaming, but they were both involved in watching a baseball game on television.

She went into the kitchen and took care of a few things, then finished setting the table. When she went back into the living room, she saw Merlin sitting on the outside of the screen door, looking in. "Hey, Sebastian, your familiar is here." She opened the door and let the cat in. He walked over to the hearth and settled down.

Sebastian looked up, saw the cat, and sighed. "What do you want now, you devil's spawn?" He looked over at Greg and shrugged. "Sorry."

"Hey, no problem. I take it he's your cat."

"No, I'm more like his person. He showed up one day and decided he wanted to live with me. I didn't seem to have any say in the matter."

"Yeah," Danni said. "And some really strange things have—"

"Danni," Sebastian said in a warning tone.

She grinned and said, "Never mind. Dinner's ready."

"Do you want to close the door to the sun room because Merlin's here?"

She shook her head. "No. Not since I've gotten to know him."

"You're not worried he'll bother the birds?"

"I don't think he will."

Sebastian shook his head. Merlin probably wouldn't dare. Apparently, Sebastian wasn't the only one entranced by Danni. His cat was as well.

After dinner Greg stood. "This was absolutely terrific, as usual, and I hate to run, but I wanted to visit Mrs. Dawson in the hospital in Norfolk before tonight's services. Sebastian"—he turned to him and held out his hand—"it's good to have you here in White Creek. I hope you find it to be as much a home as I have."

"I'm already finding I like it here very much." He managed to keep from glancing at Danni when he said it.

"You've got some good people in this town.

Honest, hardworking, loaded with southern hospitality." Gregory turned to Virgie. "Thanks again for dinner. I'll see you at the baseball game Wednesday night."

"Do you play baseball too?" Sebastian asked Virgie after Gregory had left.

"I umpire."

With Danni batting and Virgie umpiring, Sebastian decided that the baseball game was not to be missed.

His gaze turned to Danni, lingering on her golden hair. It's a shame it wasn't football, though once he got in a huddle with Danni, he doubted he'd want to come back out. And heaven only knew what would happen if he tackled her!

SEVEN

"Do you want another slice of apple pie?" Danni asked.

Sebastian set down his fork. "No, I think two was plenty. It's great, though."

Virgie got to her feet. "Well, I'm going to leave you children alone for a spell. Dot Jensen and I are going to take the altar flowers over to Mrs. Hubert's. You know she's been bedridden since she broke her hip last month." She grabbed her purse from the back of the kitchen chair and dug out her keys. She stopped by Sebastian's chair. "Sebastian, consider yourself permanently invited for Sunday dinner. You're a good-looking young thing for these old eyes to look at. Danielle, you just leave the dishes now. I'll do them later."

They did the dishes anyway, Sebastian washing, Danni drying.

This set the tone for the next couple of weeks. Danni and Sebastian worked together, watched each other, but neither was willing to discuss the desire that was always there between them. They both knew it was just a matter of time, though, before things came to a head.

Sebastian spent every Sunday afternoon with Danni and her grandmother. He discovered they usually had a house full of people—not just Gregory, but often Mrs. Walling, Lem Petrie, Magda, even Bosco Wilson and his wife. All the guests departed sometime midafternoon, then Gran, very obviously, found something to do that left Sebastian and Danni alone.

And this Sunday was no exception. "Do you want to play a game?" Danni asked when they had finished the dishes. She always suggested a game when they were alone—perhaps because the game board provided a buffer between them.

Yeah, but it probably isn't the kind of game you have in mind. Sebastian's thoughts, as usual, were all caught up with Danni. He was thinking more along the lines of contact sports. She was thinking more along the lines of checkers or gin rummy. "Parcheesi, Chinese checkers, Monopoly—do you have a preference?"

None of those. "We played Parcheesi last Sunday."

Danni's eyes gleamed. "Monopoly then. I

happen to be better at Monopoly than Parcheesi, anyway."

Sebastian sat on the sofa in the living room and flexed his knuckles. "So am I," he said in measured tones. "And you'd have to be better at Monopoly. You were lousy at Parcheesi, but I'll bet I beat you this time too."

"In that case," Danni said, "may the best man—or woman—win."

She played the game as she did everything else—wholeheartedly, enthusiastically, and with total disregard for convention. She seemed to make up rules as she went along. Sebastian enjoyed himself immensely, but then, he always did when he was with her.

This place was beginning to feel like home. *She* was beginning to feel like home. Ordinarily, he'd have worried at just how at home he felt—after all, there could be no future for them—but he felt safe letting his guard down with Danni. She'd be leaving town soon, and that in itself would end whatever was between them.

"That's two thousand bucks again," he said in satisfaction as she landed squarely on Boardwalk.

"Three times in a row," she muttered. "Who'd have thought that I'd land on Boardwalk three times in a row? I had all the greens, all the reds, all the purples, even the railroads. I should have won this game." She picked up the dice and looked at them suspiciously. "Are these loaded, by any chance?"

Sebastian leaned back and flexed his fingers, his gaze lingering on that braid of golden hair just daring him to undo it. "I'm the best, that's all. Want to try another round?"

"Not on your life. You've already beaten the socks off me once today." As if to prove her point, she stuck out her sandal-clad foot and wiggled her toes.

"Oh, come on," he urged. "One more game. I promise not to beat the socks off you again." He gave her a considering look. "We can try for T-shirts next, if you like."

She looked at him, her widened eyes all too innocent. "Why, Dr. Kent, what *are* you suggesting?"

Sebastian looked at her a long moment without saying anything, a smile playing about his lips. "How do you feel about strip poker?"

If I was sure Gran wasn't coming back for several hours—"Certainly not on Sunday!" she said, trying to sound shocked. "Could I interest you in a game of Scrabble instead?"

"Lady, you could interest me in a great many things."

The telephone rang, splitting the suggestive silence. He sighed. "But at the moment I guess you need to answer that."

She licked her lips and nodded. She came back into the room a moment later, her face sober. "It's Mrs. Kendall. Little Kevin's dog was hit by a car. They're bringing him by your office. They'll be there in a few minutes."

Sebastian immediately got to his feet. "I'll get home then. Are you coming?"

"You hurry on ahead. I'll catch up with you."

Up until now all the emergencies had been of the happier or less serious variety: An animal ready to deliver; a dog with porcupine quills in his snout; a cow with an infected udder. But this—Sebastian dashed out the door and ran down the street to his house, arriving as a rusted Ford pickup pulled up in front of his house.

Mrs. Kendall was a tall, thin brunette, currently looking harried, who held a small sobbing boy by the hand. Her husband, even taller and thinner than his wife, carried a limp bundle wrapped in an old blanket. No sooner had Mr. Kendall laid the dog on the examining table than Danni dashed in with a quick hello to the Kendalls and a comforting pat on Kevin's head.

"What can I do?" she murmured to Sebastian as he gently unwrapped the blanket from the unconscious dog.

"Prepare an I.V., then we'll have to X-ray." The dog was examined and X-rayed while the Kendalls waited anxiously. After a few minutes

Sebastian came out. He spoke a few low-voiced words to Mr. Kendall, telling him that he wasn't sure he could save the dog, but if he could, it would require extensive surgery.

"Do whatever you have to do, Doc." Mr. Kendall laid a hand on Kevin's shoulder.

Sebastian nodded, then squatted down in front of the seven-year-old boy. "You're Kevin, right?"

The boy nodded, wiping a tear away with the back of his hand. "Tuffy's my best friend, and Mom says you're gonna make him all well."

"Well, Kevin, looks like you've been a good best friend to Tuffy. I think you need to know that Tuffy has been hurt pretty badly. I don't know if I can fix him, but I promise you that I'll try very hard. I have a job for you to do. I want you to let your Mom and Dad take you home, and I want you to think about all the good times you've had with Tuffy and all the ways he's special to you. Those good thoughts will be with him when I operate. Then I'll call you later when I know how he is. Can you do that for me?"

Danni listened in the other room while she hurriedly laid out everything she thought Sebastian would need for surgery. He was so gentle and sweet with the boy that Danni found herself blinking back tears.

Sebastian came into the room. "Ready?"

"I think that's everything you'll need, but if not, let me know."

They both washed their hands in an antiseptic solution and pulled on sterile rubber gloves. Danni watched Sebastian as he worked. It was a long and difficult surgery, but he worked steadily, expertly.

His hands were quick and efficient, his eyes shadowed with concern, his brow creased. He never gave up. And Danni lost a piece of her heart.

When he was done, she asked in a soft whisper, "It doesn't look good, does it?"

He sighed deeply and shook his head. "I wish like hell I had something different to tell that little boy. He's hardly more than a baby, and he trusts me to make his best friend feel better." He sank down into a chair and leaned his head on his hands. "God, I'm tired, Danni."

She laid a hand on his head, then began stroking his hair. "All anybody can do is their best, and you did that. I stood right there beside you and watched."

"Is that going to matter to Kevin?"

"Maybe not now, but one day. And the most important thing is that you know you did your best."

His arms came around her waist, and he rested

his head against her stomach. "I'm glad you're here," he said quietly.

She cradled his head to her. "Do you want me to call the Kendalls?"

He straightened. "I'll do it."

"Sebastian, it may be all right, you know. You did what you could, God'll handle the rest. I don't know how you found that extra bleeder. You must have a sixth sense or something."

"I don't know either. Something just told me there was more bleeding somewhere. Comes from eight years as a vet, I guess." He slowly, reluctantly, got to his feet. "I'll go call the Kendalls now."

Danni laid her hand on his arm. "And I'll go see what's in your refrigerator." She gave a ghost of a smile. "You need to eat."

"I'm not hungry. Maybe later."

"It's already later, Sebastian, and you need to eat something. It's going to be a long night."

By the time Sebastian came back into the kitchen, Danni was putting together a salad from more produce old man Petrie had brought by. Canned soup already steamed in bowls on the table.

She pulled out a chair. "Sit. How'd it go?"

"He's a little kid, Danielle. He still believes in miracles, and even though I tried to explain that Tuffy might not make it, he didn't believe it. He's still expecting me to make it all right. He's expecting that miracle from me."

"If anyone can give it to him, you can."

"I'm only a man. An ordinary man who doesn't believe in miracles anymore."

Danni took the chair next to his, and her voice was as soft and warm as red velvet. "You're anything but ordinary, Sebastian Kent. You're a very, very special man. How many times am I going to have to tell you that?" She picked up the soup spoon and placed it in his hand. "Now, eat. Just a little."

He ate a few bites, more to please her than because he was hungry. Then he went back to check on the dog.

"Any change?" Danni was right behind him.

He shook his head. "I wish there were. He should have regained consciousness by now. Ordinarily, I'd be worried more about keeping an injured animal quiet so it wouldn't pop stitches or pull out the I.V."

She tugged him by the arm until he followed her into the waiting room and sat down next to her on the sofa. "You obviously care a lot about animals, but you're being too hard on yourself. Something about this one in particular is hitting close to home, isn't it?"

"Maybe I'm remembering another little boy who held a puppy in his arms and begged a doctor to make it better." He stared out the window, watching the white wings of a moth flutter against the windowpane.

"You?"

"Yeah."

"Tell me," she whispered, holding his hand in hers.

They had tried to maintain a businesslike distance the past couple of weeks, but he didn't have the energy to continue the professional veneer. And he no longer wanted to. For some reason he wanted Danni to know. He didn't like to talk about himself, but it felt right talking to her. "I was about the same age as Kevin. I had this puppy, a mutt, but it was the first thing I'd ever had that loved me blindly, thought of me first—"

"But your parents—"

"They loved me, don't get me wrong, but my mother is a research scientist who spent fifty hours or more a week at the lab. And when she was at home, she was often too preoccupied to pay a lot of attention to me. Dad is a historian, and he loves it with every fiber of his being. He's not completely alive unless he's surrounded by books and old papers. Maybe they both were, are, too self-absorbed to have had a child. I'm not sure how they ever found each other."

He clutched her hand a little harder. "I

learned to be independent early on. I even took care of paying the bills—otherwise we'd have been without heat, electricity, and a telephone. Anyway, I found this puppy one day. He was half-starved, and his fur was all matted. I took him home and fed him and bathed him, and he became my best friend. When I came home from school, finally, there was someone waiting who actually noticed I was there."

Danni's heart ached for the lonely little boy who'd had to take on responsibilities far too young. "What was your dog's name?"

He smiled. "Mike. I didn't have much of an imagination, but I always thought that Mike would make a nice brother's name."

"So what happened?" She squeezed his hands a little, as if to remind him she was right there beside him.

"He got hit by a car one afternoon. No one was there except me. I couldn't get hold of either of my parents, and I didn't know what else to do, so I picked him up and carried him to the vet. It must have been a couple of miles, I guess."

"Oh, how awful," she breathed.

"I was terrified, and I didn't have a cent on me, but I walked right into this veterinary clinic. It was past closing time, and the vet was getting into his car. I stood there and begged him to fix my dog."

"And?"

"And he took off his coat and went back to work. Mike wound up bandaged pretty much from his head to his tail, but he made it. And I kept that dog until he died of old age at seventeen. That was what made me decide I wanted to be a vet. I wanted to be able to make some other little boy's dreams stay alive.

"For the longest time after that I believed in miracles, and I wanted nothing more than to grow up and perform miracles too. Of course, I found the reality all too soon. There aren't any miracles. There's only a lot of hard work and no guarantees."

"And a lot of skill, a lot of talent, and a lot of compassion. Maybe you don't believe in miracles anymore, but I do. And I believe that people, special caring people, can sometimes make miracles happen." Her eyes told him that she didn't doubt for a moment that he was one of those people. Her unwavering faith in him helped. A lot.

She still held his hand, so Sebastian entwined his fingers with hers. He brought up his other hand and stroked it down her cheek. "Did I tell you that I'm glad you're here?"

She nodded, her cheek still cradled in his hand. "Yes, but I'd love to hear it again."

He smiled and slid his hand behind her head,

pulling her closer. "I'm glad you're here," he repeated, and grazed his lips across hers. "So glad," he said again, and slid his other hand free of hers and rested it at her waist.

He rested his forehead against hers. It felt so good to have her with him. He knew she understood. Sharon had never appreciated his love for animals, and when he'd come home depressed or angry about a patient, she'd simply snorted delicately and said, "It's just a dumb animal, Seb."

Danni sighed, and he felt her warm breath on his face. He slowly lowered his mouth to kiss her, allowing her the time to pull away if she wanted to, but she didn't. She waited breathlessly, eagerly, for the touch of his lips. And when he didn't oblige soon enough to suit her, she curled an imperious hand behind his neck and pulled his head down to hers.

As if realizing that he needed a woman's nurturing, Danni took charge of the kiss. She moved her lips over his teasingly, then ran the tip of her tongue over his bottom lip. When he reciprocated, she caught his tongue between her teeth before taking it into her mouth. She allowed her fingers to tangle in his hair as she opened her mouth to allow him better access. Her breasts felt hot and swollen, and she urged him closer, needing the pressure of his body against hers to assuage the sweet ache.

But even that wasn't enough to ease her; she needed more. She felt as if she'd been waiting all her life for this—for him. She arched her body to bring their chests even closer. Sebastian read her silent invitation for what it was and slid a hand from her shoulder, down her arm, then over her breast. He tested its weight in his hand, then smoothed his palm over the soft, full flesh.

"I never knew how empty my hands were until now." His voice was a husky whisper. "And now I know how wonderfully you fill them." *And I never knew how empty my life was until you.* He cupped her other breast, then groaned as he felt her nipples harden beneath his touch. And he needed more. He kissed her again and slid his hands beneath her short top and over the smooth bare skin of her back. He unsnapped her bra in one motion, and while his eager pirate's tongue ravaged her mouth, his greedy hands sought their treasure in the warm weight of her breasts.

"Sebastian." She whispered his name—it was a dark, sweet whisper, a greedy whisper, demanding more.

And he gave more. He found the velvet buds of her pouting nipples and rolled them between his fingers, eliciting a strangled gasp from her. He kissed her until they were both gasping for breath.

He took more. He grasped the hem of her top and pulled it up and over her head, tossing it aside as he buried his face in her neck, tasting its salty-sweetness. His teeth snagged the strap of her bra and tugged it down over her arm; then he pulled it the rest of the way off, tossing that aside as well.

He pulled back so he could see her, and Danni could feel his gaze, as intensely as though it were his fingers. It slid over her in a heated caress—touching on creamy breast and rosy nipple. "God, you're beautiful, Danielle," he breathed. "You're so beautiful. I need to taste you."

But before his lips could follow suit, they both heard a sound from the other room. It sounded like a whimper. Their eyes met, both still dazed from passion, but with a dawning awareness.

Sebastian leapt to his feet, followed by Danni, who tugged her top over her head and stuffed her arms through as she dashed behind. When Sebastian looked at the cage that he'd really believed would be the last place Tuffy would ever see, he saw the dog awake and licking at the I.V. taped to his front leg.

"I don't believe it," Sebastian murmured. "I swear I don't believe it."

Danni hugged his arm to her and leaned her head against his shoulder. "I do."

"By everything that's in me, I would have

sworn he'd never regain consciousness." He squatted down in front of the cage. "Boy, am I glad to meet you, Tuffy Kendall. And I know a little boy who's going to be delighted you're back." The dog sighed and laid its head back down, closing its eyes.

"I'll bet this is one phone call you're not going to mind making," she said.

He grinned. "This is one phone call I never thought I'd be able to make!" He glanced at his watch. "You don't suppose it's too late to call? It's after eleven."

"What would have been too late had you been waiting to hear about your puppy?"

"I get the point. I'll call."

Danni could hear him persuading an excited Kevin that his dog was asleep and needed rest and probably wouldn't appreciate a visit now. He talked to Mrs. Kendall a few more minutes, then hung up the phone. "Times like this make everything else worthwhile."

"Times like this are one of the reasons I went into veterinary medicine," Danni murmured.

"Did you really start out in art education?"

She nodded. "I love art. I love color and line and composition." She added ruefully, "I can't draw a straight line, but I loved the idea of learning all I could about art. It wasn't until I was halfway through college that I realized I needed to do something with it, so I headed for art education."

Sebastian held out his hand, and without hesitation she slipped hers into it. He led her out onto the front porch and pulled her down with him into the porch swing. He put his arm around her and pulled her close, so she laid her head against his shoulder. "And you decided not to teach?"

"Yes. Because I don't like kids in large quantities. I know I'll love my own when I have them, but since I don't intend to get married for years yet, and since I don't believe in having kids without marriage, that's not going to happen anytime soon."

That old-fashioned girl was showing again, Sebastian thought. He kept getting little glimpses of her, like the lace ruffle on a petticoat peeking below the hemline of a dress. It was out of respect for that old-fashioned girl that he was sitting on the porch swing with Danni, instead of pulling her back down onto the sofa where they'd been before Tuffy woke up. "So then you started back to school in, what was it? Business or English lit?"

"I spent a semester taking business classes, but I hated it. Then I spent a semester taking English classes before I realized that the only practical application was to teach. But I've always loved animals, and I've always been good with them. You know, I had two dogs and four cats when I was a little girl, as well as a half-dozen bunnies, I don't know how many hamsters and gerbils—they kept breeding. I started a paper route when I was eight to help pay for pet food. My dad said that anything over two dogs and four cats was unreasonable, and I'd have to help out if I wanted them."

She tilted her head back to look up at Sebastian. "What about you?"

"Mike was the only pet I had, but by the time I was ten or eleven, I was helping out at the veterinary clinic—the one I took Mike to. I did chores, like cleaning cages and feeding and walking the dogs they boarded, and they gave me twenty-five cents an hour and free veterinary care."

They talked for a long while, needing the time to let the tensions of the evening slip away. Sebastian got up only long enough to check on the dog, then settled back next to Danni in the swing. They compared notes on veterinary school, talked about their childhoods, about their first loves. Finally, Danni got up enough nerve to ask him about his marriage.

He stared off into space so long that she began to think he wasn't going to answer, but he finally said, "Her name was Sharon. I met her my last year in school. We married a few weeks after we met. I could say I swept her off her feet, but the truth is, she swept me off mine."

"What do you mean?"

"I'd been so involved in my studies that I hadn't taken out much time for a social life. Suddenly, there she was—as shiny and beautiful as a new penny."

Danni bit back a twinge of jealousy. "What went wrong?"

"I couldn't give her what she needed."

"What did she need?"

"Everything. She was the most emotionally greedy person I've ever met. She wanted everything that was inside a person but never gave anything back—not understanding, not loyalty, not even fidelity."

"Did she—was she unfaithful to you?"

Sebastian gave a short laugh. "With every guy she met. And me? I was so innocent, I never even figured it out—not until—" He took a deep breath. "Not until after the baby was born, and I found out she wasn't even mine."

"I'm sorry."

"Don't apologize for her mistakes. I don't want to talk about myself anymore. I want to know more about you. Why do you want to travel?"

Danni looked up at the stars and leaned her head against Sebastian's shoulder. "I've always lived in one place. The only time we left Raleigh was to go to the beach for a week in the summer and to come up here to visit every few weeks. I can remember, even as a little girl, looking at pictures of exotic places in books and dreaming that one day I'd go there. I'd draw pictures of mountains and palm trees, of the Eiffel Tower, the Pyramids, any place I'd never seen but had always dreamed of.

"I used to lie in the grass in my backyard and stare up at the sky, waiting for an airplane to pass over. When one did, I'd close my eyes and pretend I was on that plane. As long as I could hear the engine, I'd try to name as many places as I could. You know, something like 'My name is Danni Sullivan, and I'm going to Alaska, Bermuda, Canada, Denmark, Egypt—' "

"Finland, Georgia, Hawaii?"

"Indonesia, uh, Japan."

"What country did you come up with for *Q*?"

"Quebec."

"*X*?"

"I never got that far. Anyway, I always felt that I was so ordinary that I wanted to do something extraordinary."

He began caressing little circles on the back of her neck as they continued to talk, their conversation wandering casually from books to politics to music. Everything he found out about her only intrigued him more. Or was it the warmth of her body that intrigued him? Was it her warm, sweet fragrance?

After a while their voices trailed off, and they rocked gently back and forth in silence. He found himself toying with the end of her braid, using it to outline her ear. Finally, he began slowly to work her hair free of the plait, a strand at a time.

When he was done, he drew her hair forward over her shoulders, his fingers threading sensuously through the silken tangles. His head drew closer until she could feel the warmth of his breath. He lifted a lock of her hair, running it over his lips—feeling its texture, breathing its faint scent. "You have beautiful hair, Danielle," he murmured. "Like satin. Like sunlight."

Danni breathed in sharply as his head drew closer still, and her lashes fluttered, then closed in expectation of his kiss. When he kissed her, however, it was only the lightest brushing of his lips across hers. Then he sat back.

She opened her eyes to find him running a none-too-steady hand through his hair. "It's late, Danielle." His voice was little more than a husky whisper. "We'd better call it a night."

Danni nodded and reluctantly got to her feet. But she wasn't ready to let it drop yet. She hardly realized what she was doing as she reached out a hand and ran it down his cheek.

Sebastian gave a strained smile and grasped her hand, pressing a quick kiss to the palm before pulling it away. "If we don't stop now, I won't stop at all, sweetheart, and we're too tired. It's been a long, stressful evening, and both of us need a good night's sleep. When we make love, and it'll be soon—I think we both know that—we're both going to be well-rested. We're going to need to be."

The heat swiftly swept up her face at the images his words evoked. He was right, but that didn't make it any easier to let it go right now. But she did.

"Let me check on the dog again, and I'll walk you home."

"It's okay. You don't have to. I only live a—"

"Hop, skip, and a jump. I know. But I'll walk you home anyway."

When Sebastian came back outside, the cat was on his heels. "Where've you been tonight?" Sebastian asked.

"Maybe he's wise enough to know when to stay out of the way."

Sebastian shrugged. He wasn't going to argue about the wisdom or stupidity of his cat. He reached out and captured her hand in his, twining his fingers with hers as they slowly headed down the street. They were both silent—caught up in the maelstrom of emotions swirling around them.

They paused outside her front door, neither one quite willing to say the good night that would end the evening.

Their lips met in what was intended to be a simple good-night kiss, but there was nothing simple about it. It was, perhaps, less a kiss than a promise of things to come. Danni's legs felt as though they could barely hold her up, but her arms developed a new strength all their own as they went, without hesitation, around him, her fingers splaying over his shoulders.

"I don't understand exactly what's happening between us, Danni, but, oh, Lord, you feel so good next to me," he murmured against her lips. His restless hands swept up her back, down again, then back up to fill themselves with the yielding softness of her breasts. Danni uttered a muffled whimper of pleasure against his possessing mouth.

Sebastian very nearly lost his head at that but knew that they were both too exhausted to continue. So he pulled back a little, his hands sliding regretfully away from the warm haven of her breasts. He pressed a light kiss on her lips, her nose, her eyes, then buried his face in her hair.

With a final reluctant sigh he released her altogether. "I'll see you tomorrow."

At her dazed nod, he pressed another kiss on

her swollen lips. Her eyes held his in an eloquent plea she wasn't even aware of.

He stuffed his hands in his pockets. "Tell me good night, sweetheart," he ordered softly.

Danni gave a remarkably composed smile, considering the turmoil she felt, and replied obediently, "Good night, Sebastian."

"It was the right thing to do," he muttered to the cat as he walked back to his house. "We're both tired. She was beginning to get shadows under her eyes. I don't want to make love to her when she's more ready for sleep than passion.

"And I'm too damned tired to do it justice either. As a matter of fact, I'll probably fall asleep the second my head hits the pillow. It's after four, for Pete's sake!" But as he walked to the back room to check on the dog again, he saw a scrap of lavender lace on the floor. He picked it up. Danni's bra— low-cut and lacy, with a tiny satin bow in the middle.

He rubbed his fingertips gently over that little bow. Dammit! He'd be lucky if he slept at all.

EIGHT

Danni stopped by Sebastian's on her way to Norfolk the next morning. "How's Tuffy?"

Sebastian shook his head. "I still don't believe it, but he's doing about what I'd expect a dog with injuries half that bad to do. He even ate a little."

"I knew you could do it."

"Then you knew more than I did. But I'm glad he's doing so well."

"For the sake of little boys everywhere, hm?"

He smiled a little. "For the sake of little boys of any age. Your first class is, what, ten?"

She nodded. "It's a pretty full day."

"You'll be back around six, as usual?"

She nodded.

If he had any sense, he'd say good-bye and send her on her way. But his desire to see her overrode his good sense. And, after all, he reminded himself, it was safe. She was leaving in a couple of months. "Would you like to come here for dinner? I have a yen for a couple of grilled steaks."

Danni smiled and tried to tuck a couple of stray tendrils back into her braid. "That sounds lovely. Can I bring anything?"

Sebastian's gaze followed the movement of her hand. "Just yourself. I still have the salad you fixed last night that we never ate. Speaking of last night," he said softly, "did I thank you for being here?"

"I didn't mind, you know."

"I know." His gaze slid from her hair to her face, lingering on her lips, as if remembering the way they'd tasted last night.

Disconcerted, Danni fidgeted. "I could bring dessert."

"Dessert?"

The way he said the word spoke volumes. Danni said, "Ah, a man with a sweet tooth."

"Me?" He looked shocked. "The man who can demolish two bags of Oreo cookies in ten minutes?"

"I knew you were an Oreo-cookie man. And the dessert I have in mind is even better."

"The only thing better than Oreo cookies is sex." Sebastian's eyes glinted.

The statement hung in the air between them as brilliantly as though it were lit in neon. "Funny you should say that," she finally said, hoping the heat rising in her face wasn't apparent to Sebastian. "I thought I'd make 'better than sex' chocolate pie."

He looked at her a long moment, leaving her with the feeling that he'd not only seen the color stain her cheeks but liked it. "And is it?"

"Is what?"

"Is it really better than sex?"

Danni took a deep breath. "I guess I'd better be getting to school. I'll see you this evening."

"Oh, by the way, you left something here last night."

"What?"

In answer, Sebastian pulled the dainty lavender lace bra from his pocket and held it up by one strap.

"Oh." She grabbed the scrap of material out of his hand and hastily stuffed it into her purse.

"I'll have my new truck by the time you get home."

She tried to ignore the heat of embarrassment still suffusing her. "Oh. Um, it'll come in handy."

"It will. After all, I plan on staying in White Creek awhile, and the truck makes a lot more sense. Especially for someone who makes house calls."

Danni thought over those words as she drove into Norfolk. So he'd decided to stay in White Creek. Stay in White Creek. Her mind tiptoed around the words like a wary dog circling an unknown object. Stay in White Creek. With the Magdas, the Petries, the Bosco Wilsons, the beautification fund, the church baseball team.

Danni waited for the clutching trapped feeling she usually felt at the thought of staying, but for some reason it never came, replaced instead by a vague unsettled feeling.

She'd always thought home was a place you sent postcards to as you were en route somewhere else. But was it? Or was it a place that belonged to you, where people you loved waited to welcome you when you came home—from around the world or down the street?

She had always planned on being out of White Creek the minute she graduated. She'd figured she'd set up a nice little practice somewhere—Australia, maybe. She'd send Gran and her parents pictures of the koalas and kangaroos she'd doctored. So why didn't the image appeal to her anymore?

Sebastian. If it was true that "home is where the heart is," then White Creek was home because Sebastian was there and her heart was with him. When had she fallen in love with him, and what was she going to do about it?

Six o'clock. Danni left a note for her grandmother, telling her where she was. Of course, she had her doubts that Virgie would get home before Danni did. She was out with Lute Simpson again. And whether they drove into Norfolk for dinner and a movie or over to Waverly to a friend's, she never got home before the wee hours of the morning.

Danni didn't say anything about it. Her grandmother had been alone for twenty years, ever since her husband had died in an automobile accident. And Danni had no problems at all with her grandmother having found someone else to share her life with.

She headed to Sebastian's but walked slowly, preoccupied.

Sebastian was running late. That much was apparent as soon as Danni got to his house. There were still several cars parked on either side of a brand-new bright blue truck. She paused a moment to admire the vehicle, then walked through the waiting room, nodding hello to the people there. After she deposited the pie in the kitchen, she grabbed a white cotton jacket from the coat hook by the examining room door, slipped it on, then entered.

Beulah Barnes and Tootsie. Danni stifled a

grin. And Sebastian thought he'd seen neurotic dogs in New York! Beulah had never had children, and she invested all her maternal instincts in caring for her two Yorkshire terriers—Bootsie and Tootsie.

Sebastian saw Danni's grin and winked at her, then continued talking with Beulah. Danni could tell by the way Beulah all but preened under Sebastian's attention that he knew just the thing to say to calm the neurotic owner of two fairly normal dogs.

As soon as Beulah left, Sebastian gave a theatrical sigh and wiped imaginary sweat from his forehead. "Some character," he murmured.

Danni agreed. "She is that. Good-hearted as all get-out, but she really should have had a brood of six or seven kids to fuss over."

Sebastian nodded. "I could tell. Maybe I'll have a talk with Gregory about getting her involved in the church nursery. Her dogs will thank me for it." He nodded his head toward the door. "How many are left?"

"Only Tad Miller and his cat—he'll want you to clip Buster's claws so he doesn't destroy Tad's furniture—and John Cooper has one of his prize Bantam roosters here. I can take Tad, if you like. I've clipped Buster's claws before."

"That would be terrific. Give me a couple of

minutes before you send John Cooper in, though. I want to flip through one of my old veterinary journals and refresh my memory on chickens."

Danni opened the door and whispered over her shoulder, "Well, the first thing you should remember is to call this one a rooster, or anything else you remember won't count."

Sebastian choked back a chuckle as Danni sashayed out. He'd really missed her today. Not simply because he'd been busy nonstop since this morning either. He'd found himself missing her cockeyed way of viewing things. He'd missed the husky-sweet sound of her voice, the trill of her laughter. He'd missed her violet eyes and that odd, intriguing, aggravating twinkle in them. He'd just plain missed *her*.

The rooster had a benign growth on one foot that Sebastian took a look at before sending John Cooper on his way. As soon as he'd left, Sebastian took off the white lab coat and tossed it over the back of a chair. He couldn't wait for his evening with Danni to begin, so he peeked around the door into the waiting room to see if Danni was almost done.

Danni sat on the sofa with a cat in her lap and nail clippers in hand. Tad Miller, a huge wad of gum in his mouth, sat next to Danni on the sofa—entirely too close for Sebastian's comfort. He particularly didn't like the way Tad Miller stroked Danni's hair.

Apparently, Danni also thought Tad sat too close, because she kept inching to one side, leaving space between them, space that Tad Miller didn't hesitate to fill again. And every time he stroked her hair, she reached up and brushed his hand away. Sebastian was debating whether to go over there and punch the guy or drag him, by his neck, off the sofa and toss him out the window.

Danni looked up and caught Sebastian's thunderous expression, and her eyes plainly warned him to let her handle it. So Sebastian crossed his arms and leaned against the wall just inside the doorway—determined not to interfere, if she didn't want him to, but equally determined not to leave her alone with the gum-chewing Lothario.

He did have to admit that Danni looked especially appealing tonight—now that he had time to appreciate what she wore. She wore pink and purple again. Strange how he was getting to like that combination, especially the pink button-front dress and sheer purple stockings she wore now. His gaze lingered on her legs—the stockings fairly shouted that here were legs worth looking at. And that damn Miller fella was certainly looking.

His attention was drawn back to the couple on the sofa by Danni's sharply spoken, "Tad, I said behave yourself. I went out with you all of twice. That does not give you the right to take liberties."

Take liberties. Sebastian liked that phrase. It was such a nice, old-fashioned phrase. He hoped she was old-fashioned enough to slap Tad's face soon, because if she didn't, he was going to rip the guy's head off.

Danni said, "Tad, here, hold Buster so I can finish his claws. Oops! I need sharper clippers. I'll be back in a flash. Okay?" She got up and walked into the examining room, nearly bumping into Sebastian.

"Having problems?" Sebastian asked silkily.

"Me? Not at all. I'm almost done out there."

"Yeah. Right. I could've been done twice over by now," he teased. "You're spending more time flirting—"

Danni stuck out her tongue. "Flirting? Who's flirting? I want to get rid of him so I can eat dinner. I'm starving." She pursed her lips. "Instead of harassing me, why don't you spend a little time thinking of a way to hustle him out of here."

"What should I do? Sic the cat on him?"

Danni's eyes gleamed. "Why don't you?"

Sebastian sighed. "Right. I'm supposed to tell the cat to go in there and get Tad Miller out of here."

"Why not?"

"Danni, let's not get into that."

"Well, looks like I'll have to handle this myself then. Stand back and watch a master at work." Danni gave Sebastian a pat on the cheek and headed back to the waiting room.

"Okay, Tad. Hold Buster securely now, so I can finish this."

"Let's forget the cat awhile, Danni. Why don't we hop in my convertible and go for a drive? Gonna be a great moon tonight. I'd sure like to see it with you."

"There's no moon tonight."

"All the better then. We could spend some time alone in the dark. It's been too long since we've been alone."

"Tad, we've never spent any time alone. The first time we went out was to a public dance at the fire department. The second time was to the pizza party after the baseball game last month."

"Well, then, we're long overdue to spend time alone together."

"Drop it. I'm *not* going out with you again."

Tad released his struggling cat and grabbed for Danni's hands. Suddenly, he froze and looked down. "Damn."

"What?" Danni followed Tad's gaze. The wet streaks that ran down his jeans leg and the smug expression on Merlin's furry face said it all. She began to sputter with laughter.

She was still laughing when a disgusted Tad surged to his feet, collected his cat, and left. Only then did she realize that she was laughing alone. She looked around for Sebastian and found him staring at Merlin with a dumbfounded expression on his face.

"I see you told Merlin to get rid of Tad." She walked over to him.

Fact. "Cats are perceptive animals. Merlin obviously sensed that Tad was making a pest of himself. That's all there is to it."

"There's more to it than that, and you know it."

"Don't be ridiculous!" Sebastian muttered. "Haven't you heard of such a thing as coincidence?"

Danni leaned against the doorjamb. "Yes, I have, but don't you think the coincidences are piling on top of each other here recently?"

"You have a better explanation?"

"Yes, I do. It's magic, Sebastian. Plain and simple."

"How can you be so intelligent and yet still believe in that hogwash?"

"It's real."

"It's not."

"It is. How can you be so intelligent and yet doubt all the mysteries in the world? How can you not believe in magic or miracles?"

Sebastian grabbed her by the shoulders as if wanting to shake her. "There are logical explanations for everything. Sometimes we just don't know what they are. But they're there."

"Well, think of a logical explanation for this," Danni snapped, and reached up, threading her fingers through his hair. She urged his head down to hers and kissed him. The very second their lips touched, the sparks took over, sending the kindling into a roaring fire. When they broke apart a few moments later, their breathing was labored, their hearts pounded.

Their gazes never wavered. "Where's your logical explanation for that?" Danni asked, her voice a little shaky.

"Right out the damn window," Sebastian muttered, and hauled Danni back into his arms. His kiss was slow, hot, moist, his tongue sliding over hers, then under, before beginning a series of supremely erotic thrusts. She countered his actions with her own, opening her mouth wider, kissing him back. He let his weight press into her until she leaned back against the wall. A loud "meow" from the cat sitting on the floor next to them brought them back to reality. When Sebastian turned his heated gaze to the animal,

Merlin casually stretched and walked over to the front door.

When Sebastian didn't immediately follow him, the cat began clawing at the wood doorframe. "Fine," Sebastian muttered. "You want out? You got it." He stalked over to the door and swung it open, and the cat sauntered out, then turned back and looked at Sebastian, blinking enigmatically.

"Omigosh."

Sebastian swung his gaze to her. "What's wrong?"

"He's reminding you to lock the door."

"He only wanted to go out."

"No. He wanted to remind you to lock the door for privacy."

Sebastian did just that and walked back over to Danni. "No more talk of magic. Not now. No more talk at all."

"But, Sebastian—"

He silenced her with another kiss, then he took Danni by the hand and led her upstairs to his bedroom.

He pulled her down next to him on the bed, and his body settled over hers as he kissed her in earnest. His kiss was thorough, demanding, penetrating.

He reluctantly hauled his lips from hers long enough to drag in a ragged breath, then kissed her again. He felt as if he could kiss her forever. Her lips were soft and wet and wildly responsive.

The kid gloves were off, all walls were down, pure masculine need took over. Hardness sought softness, sharp angles sought rounded curves, demanding kisses sought total compliance. Was it possible to die of sheer need? Sebastian thought he might, as he fought for self-control. He hadn't even touched her bare skin yet, and he was already dangerously close to the edge. He squeezed his eyes shut and flung his head back, gasping in air as though he'd been drowning. Control. Control. When he thought he'd regained a smidgen, he moved a hand down the front of her dress, undoing one button at a time.

Danni moved her hands to the buttons on his shirt, but Sebastian stopped her with a groan. "Not yet, sweetheart."

"But I want to touch you."

"I don't have nearly the control that I thought I had. Please, sweetheart, let me do this my way. Later I'll be all yours."

When he finished unbuttoning Danni's dress, what he saw made his breath catch and his heart slam against his chest. She wore a skimpy purple satin slip and garter belt. If he had known she was wearing this beneath her dress instead of pantyhose, he wouldn't have let Tad Miller within a hundred feet of her.

"Are you trying to kill me?" he murmured breathlessly. "A body like yours in lingerie like this should carry an 'open at your own risk' label."

He nibbled along the low-cut neckline of the slip as he grasped the straps and pulled it down a little at a time. He pressed moist, openmouthed kisses over the swells of her breasts, then gave a convulsive swallow and drew the slip the rest of the way off.

Deliberately, he moved to cup her breasts, their warm weight filling his hands. Sebastian watched as Danni's eyes fluttered closed, and she whimpered with pleasure. His own eyes closed as he bent to kiss her again, his tongue thrusting urgently while his hands moved over her.

Her back arched in unconscious invitation, an invitation Sebastian gladly accepted when he drew one tight rosy nipple between his lips. Their hips pressed together, which helped to ease his almost painful arousal. It also made it worse. He remembered thinking that he wanted Danni to burn for him. He hadn't realized that the burning could start a fire that seared them both. And he was on fire. It burned in his gut, danced along his nerve endings, consumed all rational thought.

The clothes he still wore began to irritate his hypersensitive skin, so he rose to his feet and undressed quickly, while Danni raised up on an elbow to watch him with unabashed appreciation. When he peeled off his briefs, she breathed in sharply.

He stretched out beside her and gathered her in his arms. They both groaned as their bodies met, his hair-roughened chest fitting just right against her soft breasts. Seeking lips trailed kisses down her throat to her breasts, then down to the smooth, flat plain of her stomach. His hands slid down her hips to her thighs. He popped the fasteners loose on her garter belt and slid one stocking from her at a time, then slid the belt and panties down in one fluid movement.

Gold. He discovered gold. Delicate gold curls that protected the secrets of her womanhood. One hand slid down over her stomach, then lower still to probe gently between the folds. He replaced his hand with his lips, and Danni gasped.

Sebastian didn't know how much longer he could wait. His self-control hung in shreds, and his world had shrunk until it contained only her. The only sound was her heart beating, the only feeling that of her smoothness beneath his frantic touch, the only taste that of salt and musk and woman. He needed her desperately. More than he'd ever needed anything in his life. More than anything else in the world.

He moved back up her body, trailing kisses behind. Danni's hands fastened tightly in his hair, bringing his mouth back to hers. She could taste herself on his lips and wanted to taste him too. She reached for him, wrapping her hand around him, and shuddered when he groaned. The barest twinge of uncertainty touched her. He was so big, so powerful, she didn't know how she'd ever be able to accept him. And yet, she didn't think she'd survive another minute if she didn't.

"Sebastian," she whispered. "Now. Love me now."

He moved his body over hers, his legs slipping between her thighs and urging them apart. "Protection," he gasped. "Sweetheart, are you protected?"

Danni took a deep breath and tried to focus her scattered thoughts. "Not—not at the moment."

Sebastian left her just long enough to dash into the bathroom. He came back, setting a box on the nightstand.

"A whole box?"

"We can get more, if we need them."

He stretched out next to her and groaned at the feel of their bodies pressing together. He felt as if he could make love to her a hundred times, and it wouldn't assuage the hunger inside. He took care of the protection, then moved back into her frantic embrace. He slid a finger inside, to see if she was ready. She was so hot and wet and tight that he nearly exploded right there.

She arched her hips against his probing. "It'll kill me if you don't take me now," she pleaded. "I need you."

Sebastian bit the inside of his lip. Hard. The moment of pain gave him just enough control back that it enabled him to go slowly. He moved into her slick heat until he hit a barrier. He paused in shock. "What?"

"Don't stop," Danni hissed.

"Danni—"

"Now, please. Now." She wrapped her legs around him and rocked her hips up, drawing him in deeper. One final sharp thrust broke him through.

"Are you okay, sweetheart?" He sighed heavily, and she nodded. Their bodies rocked together endlessly, timelessly. Danni's hands slid down his back to his hips, holding him tighter against her. She could feel Sebastian trembling as he tried to be gentle, for her sake, his body taut and covered with a fine sheen of sweat. But she didn't want gentle anymore. She wanted wild. She wanted primitive. She wanted as much as she could take and then some.

Heat radiated through her, and she gasped as the whole world seemed to become one giant ball of light. She closed her eyes against the blinding light that grew until she felt it seep into her very pores. Shudders of ecstasy shook her again and again, and she muffled her cries against his shoulder.

Only when her soft cries subsided did Sebastian thrust hard and fast, his body convulsing as he rocketed over the edge after her.

Reality drifted back slowly. Long minutes passed before Sebastian lifted his head and smiled down at her. "Are you okay, sweetheart?"

Danni smiled and nodded. "Perfect."

"It was that."

"Yes, but that's how I feel, too."

He slid a lazy hand over her breast. "I agree. You do feel perfect." His face sobered. "Why didn't you tell me?"

"Tell you what?" Danni murmured against the warm skin of his shoulder.

"That you were—you were a virgin."

"That's not something you can toss out in normal conversation, you know." Danni smiled drowsily. "Gee, Sebastian, Mrs. Walling is waiting to see you, and by the way, did you know I'm a virgin?"

"You should have told me tonight then."

"When? During our argument? Or later, when our mouths were occupied with each other?"

"You still should have told me."

She opened her eyes and looked up at him. "Would it have made a difference tonight if I had?"

Sebastian fell silent. Would it? Probably not. He'd been too far gone—eaten up with desire. "I don't know," he finally said. "Maybe not."

He felt a pang when he thought of what a responsive and unselfish lover she'd been and of what she'd given him. Her first time.

Guilt crept inside him. Suspicion followed close on the heels of guilt. Why him? Why had she chosen to give her virginity to him? Was she going to want something in return?

This was a mistake. He should never have allowed things to progress this far. And yet he wasn't sure he'd have been able to stop them. He and Danni were like kerosene and a match. Innocuous enough by themselves, but together they created an earth-shattering explosion. An upheaval.

And Sebastian didn't want any more upheavals in his life. He'd had plenty. Peace and calm. A quiet, settled country life. These were things he'd craved—things he'd come here looking for. And Danni? She wanted out of here. She'd be heading out of White Creek before the end of the summer. And it was just as well.

Not getting involved with her was easier said than done though. Every cell in his body craved joining with hers. He woke up in the mornings looking for her to be there and went to bed at night to dream of her. And after the lovemaking they had shared, not getting involved was going to be next to impossible. But this was an ill-fated relationship at best. She believed in magic, for heaven's sake. And he didn't.

NINE

"Why me, Danni? Why did you wait for me?"

Danni wondered if he knew how afraid he looked? Was he afraid that she was going to start weeping and demand he marry her or something? Even if, in her deepest heart, she had wanted to do that, she had too much pride. After all, she'd been the one to say there would be no strings. Had her words come back to haunt her?

She'd better let him know he was off the hook and fast before he dashed out of the bedroom. "What makes you think I waited for you?"

Apparently, that wasn't what Sebastian expected her to say, because his eyebrows rose in surprise. "Then why—" He stopped short, not sure how to continue.

"Why did I sacrifice my virginity so easily?"

Was that the right touch of nonchalance in her voice? "Maybe I considered my virginity something I'd be better off without." *And maybe I'm lying through my teeth.*

She watched as he pondered this statement, a muscle working in his cheek. He didn't seem pleased with what she said. She was glad.

"So I was as good as anybody?"

"I wouldn't say that. Based on my experience, limited, of course, I'd say you were better than most." She smiled too innocently.

"Thanks," he murmured, sounding as if he wasn't sure if he was amused or not. "Danni, I'd really like to know. You held on to your virginity so long. Why did you give it up now?"

She sighed. "I wanted you. It seemed like the right time."

"And it had never seemed like the right time before?"

"No, it hadn't."

"But"—he paused for a moment trying to come up with precise words—"we did say no strings—"

"Sebastian, I gave up my virginity. I didn't propose marriage. Don't worry. I said no commitments, and I meant it. I'm not suddenly going to turn prim and proper on you and demand you do the honorable thing by me. My virtue, if you will, was mine to give. And I chose to give it to you. End of story. I don't ask for a darn thing in return. Nor do I expect it."

Perhaps that's what made him feel most guilty of all. And because he felt guilty, he decided to give her the one thing he could—a night so memorable, she'd never, ever forget it. And he'd start by loving every single inch of her body from her head to her toes.

With their naked bodies pressed together, Sebastian knew Danni could feel his renewed arousal pressing intimately against her. But he did nothing about it. Instead, he concentrated on her face. He brushed the tip of his tongue over her eyelashes, drew her bottom lip gently between his teeth, sucked on her earlobe. He pulled long strands of her hair over her face and kissed her through them. He brushed her hair away and kissed her again. And again and again.

Danni kept trying to urge him to do more, but he resisted. He was going to love her so completely, so thoroughly, that forever after she wouldn't be able to get the feel of him out of her pores. And why he needed to mark her so completely as his, he wouldn't think about now. When he finally left her mouth, he moved to her throat, nibbling, kissing, sucking.

"Sebastian," Danni pleaded, her voice thready

with need, "you promised next time would be mine."

"The rules just changed, sweetheart. You'll get your turn later."

When Danni tried to move her hands on him, Sebastian easily fastened them above her head, out of his way. He continued to move slowly downward. He spent long, delicious moments sucking her beaded nipples. Every soft whimper of pleasure that passed through Danni's lips made his shaft move with a life of its own.

He released her hands as he pressed kisses down the silky-smooth skin of her abdomen. Her hands clutched at his head, trying to pull him up to her. But when his lips found the tiny bud of her womanhood, her clutching hands held him to her instead. She tossed her head back and forth, her breath coming in short gasps. But when she reached the pinnacle, he didn't let her fall into sweet pleasure. Instead, he moved his lips to the insides of her thighs, the backs of her knees, the instep of her tiny foot. She arched her hips beneath his; she dug her fingernails into his shoulders; she pleaded, but to no avail.

Finally, with quick, agile strength, she slid her body from beneath his and, catching him by surprise, pushed him onto his back. Her eyes were lit with a feverish glow as she smiled a supremely wicked smile. "Turn about is fair play, my dear. Your damnable self-control is getting on my nerves, and I'm going to make you lose it."

She straddled his body with her own and bent down, running the tip of her tongue around his flat brown nipple, then pulling the small, hard tip between her teeth. When he groaned, she did the same to the other nipple, then ran her hands down over his stomach. Her light, feathery touches tickled, caressed, stroked, until his entire body tightened with his need.

"Danni! You win," he gasped, and rolled over, pinning her beneath him. "I have no control left." He lost his breath entirely as she took him inside. His hands lifted her hips toward him as he delved deeper, harder. Hands clasped hands, tongues danced and mated, warm dark whispers mingled, bodies spiraled together toward the sharp pleasure-pain of ecstasy.

They muffled their cries of fulfillment against each other as the jolts of pleasure went on and on. Finally, Sebastian collapsed on top of her, his body limp and empty. He'd wanted to imprint himself on her, and he had. But in doing so, she'd imprinted herself on him, as well.

He dragged in one ragged breath, then another, and reality began to trickle in. Her heart pounded as hard and fast as his did. And their bodies were still joined. He couldn't bear to break loose. But she was such a delicately built thing that he also didn't want to crush her, so he angled his body to one side, keeping his arms around her and holding her as close as two people could get. She sighed a little and nestled her head on his shoulder. Finally, enough reality trickled in that he realized one very important fact. "Damn!" He propped up on an elbow.

Danni opened a sleepy eye. "Hm?"

"Danni, I haven't done a very good job of taking care of you, I'm afraid."

"You took care of me just fine," she murmured silkily.

"No, sweetheart, I didn't. I, ah, I forgot to use any protection that time."

Her other eye flew open, and she stared up at him as she did some rapid mental calculation. Finally, she said, "It's okay."

He stroked her hair back from her face. "Are you sure?"

She stared off into space and redid her calculations. "Positive."

"You'd let me know if—if anything happened?"

"Of course I would, but it won't." *I hope.*

She tried not to feel too hurt when she heard his sigh of relief. Was the idea of having a tie to her so horrible?

Pregnant. In the past when she'd thought of being pregnant, she'd always felt trapped. And she waited for the feeling now—sure it would come. But it didn't.

Instead, she felt a strange stirring deep inside, a warm, pleasant feeling at the thought of holding a baby. A baby with Sebastian's eyes and melting smile. Or was it the thought of any baby? She imagined another baby, Tad's or Gregory's. Cute babies, but no strange little flutters at the thought. So it was definitely the idea of Sebastian's baby that did it. And that scared her more than anything else. After all, he didn't want commitments, and a baby was the biggest commitment of all. And if he even suspected what she was thinking, he'd be out of here like a shot.

She shivered, and he wrapped his arms around her even more tightly. After a few minutes he stood and pulled her up next to him. "C'mon." He led her by the hand into the bathroom and turned on the water, filling the tub.

"What's this for?" she asked curiously.

"Your sore—uh—bottom."

"My sore . . . ? Oh." She smiled up at him. "It's not that sore, you know."

"But the warm water will feel good."

"And that huge tub will feel lonely. Have you noticed, Sebastian, that these wonderful old-fashioned tubs are big enough for two?"

She smiled and ran her fingertip around a flat brown nipple. It puckered satisfyingly.

He caught his breath and released it. "Yeah, I'd noticed."

"So?" She stepped into the water and smiled up at him invitingly.

"So." He stepped into the water after her and pulled her into his arms.

Water was everywhere when they were done—the rug on the floor soaked, the towels wet. He leaned back in the tub, his eyes closed, Danni in his arms. Another first. He'd never taken a bath with someone before—not that bathing had been on either of their minds.

Twice now, he'd made love to her without protection. Safe time or not, this was taking too many chances. What was there about her that knocked all good sense out of his head? He'd *never* before forgotten something as important as protection. However, she made him forget all about things like responsibility. And that he couldn't afford to do. Maybe this was the biggest reason they should never have gotten involved.

They managed to make it from the bathtub to the bed, where Danni lay cradled in Sebastian's embrace. Thoughts whirled through his head

Oh, hell. He was involved with her up to his earlobes—and he didn't want to be. He suddenly realized just how hard it was going to be to let her go, even knowing that a relationship between them could never survive. He was going to have to stop this before it went any further.

"Well, um, I'm sure you'll be wanting to get home soon. Before your grandmother worries."

"Hm?" She wasn't sure she'd heard him correctly.

"I, uh, said that you'll probably be wanting to leave soon so your grandmother doesn't worry."

She could take a hint, especially when it was more than a hint, it was just short of a kick out the door. "Yes. You're right. I wouldn't want to worry Gran. I'll get dressed and go home."

Danni didn't tell him her grandmother wasn't even at home. His voice sounded strained to her, as if he were regretting what happened. And his suggestion was certainly lame enough that it was obvious he was looking for a way to get her to leave without actually saying so.

She dressed quickly and in silence—the most uncomfortable silence she'd ever experienced. It was as if they no longer knew what to say to each other. After making love three incredibly intimate heart-stopping times, they were uncomfortable with each other.

It was painfully clear to her that he really

had bought her "no-strings" spiel lock, stock, and barrel. He was a sensitive and caring man—about most things—and if he knew she'd changed her mind about all that, he'd feel bad. Guilty. Worse yet, he'd feel responsible. So she pasted on a bright smile as she finished buttoning her dress. "We never did get to dinner, you know."

Sebastian, who was tugging on his jeans, said, "I could still grill those steaks, if you like."

"Ah, no. I—I don't want Gran to worry."

He nodded. "Right. I'll walk you home then."

"It's not necessary." If he did, he'd see that Gran's car was gone. "I'll see you later." While he was still zipping his pants, she stuffed her feet into her shoes, grabbed her stockings and garter belt from the floor, and all but ran down the stairs.

Sebastian sat back on the edge of the bed. "Well, she couldn't wait to get out of here," he muttered to the cat who sat on the windowsill, tail twitching. He managed to overlook the fact that he'd all but ushered her out.

He had her wishes at heart, he told himself. She wanted to leave White Creek, and he wanted her to be able to go with a clear conscience. Tell the truth, a little voice inside him insisted. Aren't you afraid that if you made love with her one more time, you wouldn't be able to let her go at all?

Her body ached in delicious secret places. Had life been fair, she should have been cuddled in Sebastian's arms, letting his body's warmth soothe the ache. Instead, she cuddled the pillows on her overstuffed love seat, staring across the darkened room and feeling unutterably lonely.

She felt like a homeless child—ironic when she considered that she'd spent most of her life waiting until she was old enough to leave home. But now she couldn't dredge up any enthusiasm for any of her old fantasies. The veterinary practice in Hawaii, for example, with its palm trees, blinding sands and the sulfuric fumes of the volcanoes. Then, somehow, she conjured up pictures of Sebastian making love to her on those sands.

Wrong fantasy. She jerked her thoughts to Australia instead. Only now Sebastian made love to her in full view of the curiously watching kangaroos.

No, the fantasies she liked the best were the ones set right here in White Creek—some were things they'd done, others things she'd wished for. Sitting next to Sebastian in church, their thighs pressed together. Her playing outfield to his third base at the baseball games. Sitting up with him when he spent the night watching over an injured animal. Playing silly games with him on Sunday afternoons, biding time until night fell and they were alone to pursue more interesting activities.

"Well, damn. I've gone and done it now, haven't I?" she murmured, but the two dozing mynah birds in the corner never even twitched a feather.

She was grounded, flightless, her wings clipped, and she could even imagine she felt the weight of a ball and chain around her ankle. But she no longer cared, because she didn't want to leave anymore. She wanted to stay here. With Sebastian.

She loved him. For someone who'd never wanted anything tying her anywhere, she suddenly wanted strings, twine, yarn, rope. Chains. She wanted anything that would tie her irrevocably to Sebastian Kent. And wasn't it ironic that the woman who'd spent her whole life avoiding commitment should want it now—but with a man who didn't? She didn't even notice she was crying until a large teardrop landed on her hand.

It's not fair. Tonight was so wonderful! It seems I've waited my whole life for it. I did wait my whole life for it. And what happens? He hurries me home so I won't worry Grandma. Is he so afraid of commitment that he couldn't even give me one whole night? If that's the way he wants to be, then I'll just pretend tonight never happened.

Fat chance!

Tuesday afternoon Danni showed up at Sebastian's promptly at one o'clock with a list of house calls to make. She wanted to throw herself into his arms but instead gave him an impersonal smile. "You ready to go?" she asked with determined cheerfulness.

He gave a brusque nod, not quite meeting her eyes. "Let me get my bag."

The easy camaraderie between them was gone. Danni could have wept. They really needed to discuss what happened—or didn't happen—last night, but Danni would die before being the one to bring it up.

One minute everything had been fine, the next there had been a major emotional withdrawal on his part—right after he'd made love to her that last time. It was if he'd suddenly realized—realized what? That he didn't want to be involved after all? That he'd enjoyed making love the first two times, but not the third?

That it was getting too close for comfort? Danni watched Sebastian through lowered lashes as he drove. She had a feeling that was closer to the truth. Maybe he'd realized that he *was* getting involved, at least a little bit. Or maybe he'd realized that she was getting involved a lot.

Things got worse as the day went on. It got to the point where they only talked to each other when absolutely necessary and then only in monosyllables. It came to a head when they made a late afternoon call to Magda's. She seemed to be immediately aware of the palpable tension between the two of them.

She nodded her head in Sebastian's direction and removed the stem of the corncob pipe from her mouth. "You shoulda been wearing blue, like I told you."

"Don't bother, Magda," Danni said. "He doesn't believe in that."

"Well, then, he should. The two of you oughta be married by now."

"Married!"

"Married?"

Both Danni and Sebastian responded at the same time.

"That's what the cat was for. I talked to my grandma, and she said a six-toed cat with two-color eyes means romance."

"That's a bunch of hogwash," Sebastian said forcefully. "We're not about to get married." He added for good measure, "No way!"

"You don't have to sound so horrified at the idea," Danni muttered.

"I don't want there to be any misunderstandings."

"Oh, there won't be," Danni said. "You've made your feelings perfectly clear."

"I thought the feelings were mutual. *You* were the one who said there would be no strings."

"Go ahead, throw my words back in my face. I'm allowed to change my mind, if I want to."

Sebastian stopped dead. "Did you?"

"Did I what?"

"Did you change your mind?"

"What if I did? Huh?"

Sebastian half turned away. "You said you were leaving this summer. You were the one who went on and on about no commitments, no ties. And I told you *I* didn't want any. I know I told you."

"Did I ask you for commitment?" Danni shouted. "I only want what's freely given, and getting a commitment out of you would be like pulling teeth."

Magda interrupted. "Could I say something here?"

Sebastian snorted. "I don't want to hear any more talk about colors. You've already got Danni convinced—"

"Nobody convinces me of anything, Dr. Kent." Danni bit off the words. "I'm a big girl, and I've been making my own decisions for years. And you know what I've decided? I've decided you're in a rut. You're in a rut so deep, you can't see out."

"Can't see what? All the unexplainable things you believe in? I'm not in a rut. My life is logical and orderly because that's what makes sense."

"That's what makes boring."

"*This* is why a relationship between us would never work. We'd never agree on anything."

"I haven't asked you for a relationship. And do you know why? It's because I know you're not capable of it. And you're not capable of it because you're terrified. Terrified!" Her fists were clenched so tightly at her sides that her knuckles stood out white. "I'm going home now." She nodded in Magda's direction. "Magda, I'll see you later. I'll take the creek, if you don't mind." Without a backward glance at Sebastian she left.

Magda turned her keen gaze on Sebastian. "Bad thing to go against what was meant to be. Blue goes real good with pink and purple." She stuffed her pipe back between her teeth and tucked her hands in her pocket, then turned away. "They're the colors of a sunrise," she said over her shoulder.

It was just as well, Sebastian told himself as he drove home. He had nothing left to give to a relationship. And the two of them were certainly the century's most mismatched pair. He'd made the right decision not to get any further involved with her.

So if it was the right decision, why did he feel so empty inside? He felt as if she'd taken all his emotions with her—all his energy, all his enthusiasm, all his laughter.

He stared at the ceiling most of the night. The bed suddenly seemed too big, too empty. The mattress itself seemed to remember Danni and the impression of her body. And the pillowcase smelled of her hair.

He went downstairs and stretched out on the sofa, only now he found himself thinking about sitting here with her after the emergency surgery. He remembered how glad he'd been she was here and that she understood. Damn.

Sebastian went out to the porch and sprawled in the swing. There, that was better. The cool night breeze would blow thoughts of her right out of his head. But it didn't work that way. The last time he'd sat in the swing, Danni had been close beside him, head on his shoulder. His shoulder seemed to remember the exact weight of her head.

Why couldn't the woman stay out of his house? Why couldn't she stay out of his head? Why couldn't she stay out of his heart?

She wondered if he were having as much trouble sleeping as she was. Probably not. The dull and stodgy slept like tops. She sighed. Unfortunately, Sebastian wasn't really dull and stodgy. Why did he pretend to be?

Why couldn't he realize that they belonged together? She could see it as clearly as if it were a divine revelation. Or was she the only one who saw it? Maybe he couldn't see the magic, because it wasn't there for him.

She inhaled sharply, and her eyes stung. There was the truth she'd been avoiding. It was entirely possible that he really didn't feel any more for her than he would for anyone who'd been a pleasant diversion. After all, she'd set the ground rules herself. And it wasn't his fault that she'd broken them.

Maybe she only thought she saw the love in his eyes because she was looking through the love in her own. She thought back over the past twenty-four hours. All of his actions pointed to the one thing, the one horrible gut-wrenching thing, she hadn't wanted to admit. He didn't love her.

But knowing him as she did, he had to be aware of her feelings for him, though perhaps he wasn't aware of the depth or the magnitude.

And he would feel bad for her, even guilty. He'd pile all the blame on himself because she had been a virgin, and he would assume that he'd taken advantage of her innocence. She'd never be able to convince him she'd given it freely.

She hated the idea of Sebastian feeling somehow responsible for her. Worse yet, suppose he felt sorry for her? She wanted to recoil in horror from the thought. If Sebastian were a different kind of man, a less honorable one perhaps, he would take pleasure in remembering his conquest. Sebastian would take no such pleasure. He'd tear himself up over it—unless Danni did something to stop that.

She sat up in bed, wiping away the silent tears that persisted in squeezing out, and put her mind to work.

The next morning she pasted on a bright smile and arrived at Sebastian's about five minutes to nine. Sebastian looked somewhat surprised to see her.

"Hello," he said quietly, almost diffidently.

"Hi," she chirped, handing him a cup of coffee. "It's decaf. That's all Gran made this morning. She said she didn't need caffeine."

"Thanks. Uh, Danni—"

"You said yesterday to remind you that you needed to run by John McLendon's and check on those two foals. You also said you wanted to run by Lem Petrie's and check on Sal's hoof."

"Danni?"

"Oh, and Mel Raines wants you to drop by sometime too."

"Danni."

"What?"

"About yesterday—"

"Yeah, I need to apologize. I lost my temper."

"We both lost our tempers, but since nobody's due in for another few minutes, I think we need to talk."

Danni perched on the arm of the sofa and crossed her arms in front. She schooled her features into what she hoped looked like an expression of mild interest. "About what?"

"About you, me." He took a deep breath. "I think that you . . . I think that you might have—"

"Fallen in love with you?" Danni interrupted. "So?"

"What do you mean 'so'?"

"So what? I don't expect anything from you, if that's what you're worried about," she stated simply.

"But you have every right to. I took your virginity, for heaven's sake."

"I *gave* it. There's a difference."

"Not much. It still makes me responsible for—"

"It makes you responsible for nothing. I am over the age of consent." She paused and looked directly at him. "I'm not embarrassed by my feelings for you, Sebastian. Anyway, I'm sure they'll eventually go away—sort of like a case of measles, don't you think? It makes you uncomfortable for a while, then they go away."

"Falling in love with me is like a case of measles?"

"Yeah."

Measles? Sebastian ran a hand through his hair and tried again. "Danni, I'm sorry about the way this all worked out. I guess I assumed you, uh, knew the score before we—I—"

"Made wild, passionate love?" Danni supplied helpfully.

Uncomfortable, Sebastian shifted position. "Something like that. Anyway, I think we both know that this no-strings thing isn't going to work between us, so I think we should try, try to keep our, uh, relationship—"

"Professional?"

"Yeah. Professional. We're two mature, responsible people, and I'm sure we—"

"I can't."

"You can't?"

"I can't be responsible and professional around you."

"You're doing a damn good job of remaining

cool and calm right now!" Sebastian muttered, disgruntled.

"It's not as easy as it looks. What did you want? Did you want me to throw myself at your feet and beg you to marry me?"

"Well, no, but—"

"You'd never get that from me. But you look at me like you keep expecting me to do just that. And that's one of the reasons why I'm giving you notice."

"Notice!"

"When I graduate next week, I'm going to take a temporary job, for the summer only, at a clinic in Kennebunkport, Maine."

"You're leaving?"

"Don't sound so surprised. You knew I would sometime, didn't you? It's just a little sooner than I planned."

"Danni, I know we can work something out. Don't let me chase you away."

Danni raised her eyebrows with cool hauteur. "Don't flatter yourself, Dr. Kent. You're not chasing me away. I'm choosing to go because I don't like hitting my head against brick walls."

"Brick walls? What are you talking about?"

"If I stayed in town, I'd be sorely tempted to try to convince you what a coward you are."

"I'm not a coward."

"Aren't you? You should have seen your face

the other night when you asked me why I chose you to"—she pursed her lips—"deflower me, if you will. Your face was a study in abject terror. You were so afraid I was going to profess my undying love and chase you around begging you to marry me."

"I was not afraid. I just didn't want any tears or hysterics or anything."

"Sebastian," Danni said dryly. "I'm hardly the hysterical sort. And it wasn't that you were afraid of. You were afraid that I might shake you out of the safe little rut you've gotten so comfortable in."

"I'm not in a rut."

"You are too. Anyone who can't entertain new ideas is in a rut."

"If you're talking about magic again, then I—"

"Don't want to talk about it, right? That's your answer to everything. If you don't talk about it, you can pretend it doesn't exist."

"I don't want to argue."

"Neither do I. I'm taking the day off." Danni stood, grabbed her purse, and headed out.

"Wait a minute!" Sebastian followed her to the door. "You can't go marching out of here in the middle of an argument."

"Watch me."

TEN

That performance should qualify her for an Oscar, Danni thought as she collapsed into a boneless heap on her sofa. Her voice had been steady, her knees securely locked, even her hands hadn't trembled. No, the shaking was all on the inside. She hadn't quite figured out yet whether she was shaking from the force of unshed tears—or with the desire to get her hands around Sebastian's neck.

She was less brokenhearted than angry, she realized, though she knew the heartbreak was right beneath the surface. Right now, though, she was furious at the man for being too blind to see how good they were together.

But she had too many things to do in her life to waste time acting as a pair of eyeglasses for a man who couldn't see what was right in front of his nose. So she stiffened her knees and stood. She had a lot of studying to do before exams.

She had just spread her books and papers out and was trying desperately to focus her mind on what she was doing, when there was a tap at the front door. Danni peeked into the living room and saw Sebastian silhouetted on the other side of the screen.

Her acting ability was good but not great. If he didn't leave her alone soon, she was going to crumble into little pieces at his feet. She forced a smile and spoke through the screen. "Don't you have patients to see?"

"I don't want to leave things the way we did."

"Why not?" She made the mistake of looking up then and meeting his eyes. Sweet heaven, she'd missed his eyes. She wanted to crawl into his walnut-brown gaze and never come out again. She lowered her own gaze to the floor. If she looked any longer, she was afraid she'd do the one thing she said she'd never do—throw herself at his feet and beg him to marry her.

He pushed at the screen door, but the hook at the top was fastened. "Can I come in and talk?"

"You have a job to do, and I have studying to do. That job in Kennebunkport isn't a shoo-in. I still have to pass my exams."

"Danni, I—"

She tilted her chin up, managing to lift her gaze as high as the neck of his shirt. "Look, what the hell do you want from me, Dr. Kent? What is it you want me to say or do?"

He looked down at his feet and shook his head helplessly. "I wish I knew."

"When you do know, come see me. Until then, I have more pressing things to do." She turned and walked back into the sun room. He knocked again, but she ignored it.

"Danni?"

She didn't answer. She stood in the middle of the room, waiting for him to leave, her eyes squeezed shut against the burning tears that threatened to fall. Every nerve in her body had been stretched to the breaking point. For God's sake, leave! she implored silently. She relaxed her body only after she heard his footsteps fading away.

She'd go on without him. That was the way she was, but she knew that a lot of her innate enjoyment of life would be gone. She'd never again be able to look at things with the same wonder and excitement—and all because she'd loved and lost a man like Sebastian Kent. No, she hadn't lost him. She'd never even had him.

She'd meant it when she told Sebastian that she'd get over him just like the measles. Unfortunately, she had a feeling it was going to be one horribly long convalescence. With a sigh she sank back down onto the sofa with her books and spent the next two hours blotting tears and making notes.

Damn her hide! Things were all screwed up, and it was her fault. She swept into his life, bringing color and confusion and delightful disorder in her wake, and made him not only get used to it but learn to like it. And then she said she was going to leave town and take it all away with her.

He had a steady stream of patients, but his day still seemed quiet and slow and infinitely dull. Everywhere he looked there was that damned cat of his staring him down with an accusatory glare. By the end of the day he'd thought about tossing the cat off the roof—and jumping after him.

He felt unaccountably edgy—as if someone had rubbed his nerves with sandpaper. He decided a walk might settle him down, and if he headed in Danni's direction, it was only because there was a large patch of wildflowers beside the road down that way he wanted to check out. It had nothing to do with hoping to catch a glimpse of her.

Her Jeep was gone. He told himself he'd only noticed because it was hard to miss the absence of the bright red vehicle. And when he headed to her front door, it was only because he wanted to say a neighborly hello to Virgie Pace. He certainly had no intention of pumping her for information about Danni.

So why were the first words out of his mouth "Is Danni really leaving for Maine?"

"Hello to you too, Dr. Kent." Virgie Pace took off her black leather hat and scratched her head.

"Sorry," Sebastian mumbled, embarrassed. "How are you?"

"Fine, but the real question is how you are. You don't look so hot to me. What happened to your hair?"

Sebastian knew his hair was standing on end; he'd tunneled his fingers through it dozens of times today—every time he thought about Danni leaving, in fact. "I slept on it wrong."

"Mm-hm." She didn't sound convinced. "Funny, by the size of the bags beneath your eyes, I'd have said you haven't slept at all."

"I had a restless night. Is Danni really going to Kennebunkport?"

"As far as I know."

"When is she leaving?"

"The day after her graduation."

He nodded and fell silent, finally murmuring, "I wonder what it would take to induce her to stay."

"I don't think money figures into it."

Sebastian stuffed his hands in his pockets. "I guess not. I, uh, have some things to take care of. I'll see you later." Slowly, he walked away.

Virgie went back inside. "There goes one unhappy camper."

Danni looked up. "There's nothing I can do about that, Gran. It's all up to him."

"You don't *have* to leave White Creek, you know."

"Yes, I do. I can't stay. I'll get over this, Gran, I know I will, but not here. In a town this size I'll be seeing him nearly every day. And what about my own veterinary practice? Even if I worked out of a clinic in Norfolk or Portsmouth, I'd still see him at church or baseball or merely walking down the street." She hit her fist against the arm of the sofa. " I wish we didn't live so close."

"You've never been one to run away, Danielle."

"I'm not running away now either. I'm not. I'm only giving myself a little time and space. I'll be back at the end of the summer—for a little while, anyway. How long I stay then depends on, well, on how I feel about—you know."

Virgie sat next to her granddaughter on the

sofa. "I guess some men are deaf, dumb, and blind when it comes to love, Danielle."

Danni gave herself over to her grandmother's comforting embrace and sighed. "And some men are just dumb."

Another sleepless night. Sebastian had had an emergency house call, but that had been early in the evening. Still, that on top of what seemed to have been an ungodly long day left him feeling exhausted.

He changed the sheets on the bed in case a trace of her fragrance still lingered. Not that it had done any good. Simply because no trace of her scent lingered physically didn't matter. The aroma was engraved on his memory. Still, he had high hopes that he'd actually be able to get some sleep.

After two hours of tossing and turning, he sat up. He'd be able to sleep if it were cooler, he knew it. He got up and opened the window. There, that would make all the difference in the world.

He lay on his left side and stared at the wall, then flopped over onto his right side to stare at the glowing red numbers on his clock. Finally, he sat up again. The damn bed was too big. That was the problem. It was simply too big—

and too empty. He sighed and resigned himself to another sleepless night where Danni haunted his every thought.

He finally dozed off before dawn, but even then, he dreamed about Danni. He dreamed they'd made love again and again before finally falling asleep in each other's arms. Where they belonged.

He awoke with his arms around Merlin. Sebastian opened his eyes to find the cat watching him with what Sebastian would have sworn was amusement. "Sorry, fella, you're no substitute for her," Sebastian muttered as he gently pushed the cat to one side. The cat jumped to the windowsill and looked back at Sebastian with a haughty look.

"Fine, so I have only myself to blame if she's not here. Is that what you're trying to tell me? What the hell am I supposed to do about it?"

Sebastian got to his feet and put on his trousers. "She's driving me nuts. Not only can I not sleep, but now I'm talking to you as if I expect you to answer me."

The cat meowed and closed his eyes, and Sebastian sighed. He needed to talk to Danni. Right now. He had no idea what he was going to say to her, though, so he'd have to wing it. Wing it. He hadn't done much of that in his life. Up until now he'd always had things planned out.

But Danni refused to let herself fit into any set of plans.

He pulled on a shirt and stuffed his feet into shoes. When he arrived at Danni's, her Jeep still wasn't there. He was about to turn and leave when he saw the glint of sunlit gold in the backyard. Danni. He walked to the back gate.

"Hi."

She looked up from the tray of bedding plants she was kneeling over. "Hi."

She looked beautiful. Her hair was tied at the nape of her neck with a violet-blue scarf the same color as her eyes. His gaze lingered on the expanse of leg revealed by the snug cutoff jeans, then moved upward to caress the lush breasts outlined by the pink T-shirt she wore. He could remember in infinite detail the way they felt in his hands or crushed against his chest, the way they tasted. A pang shot through him. He missed her. Right down to his soul.

"I wasn't sure you were here," he finally said. "Your Jeep is gone."

"It's at the Texaco having a little work done before I leave. How are you?"

"I—it's been busy. We work pretty well together, you and I. I really—need you. I wish—I wish you'd come back."

She shook her head and looked down at the poor little marigold plant she'd mangled between her fingers. "I'm sorry." She looked back up at him. She'd never seen Sebastian look like this. His hair hadn't been combed, his trousers were wrinkled as if he'd forgotten to carefully hang them up as usual. His shirt was not only buttoned wrong but wasn't even tucked in. And, wonder of wonders, he'd forgotten to put on his socks. She was still pondering this when her thoughts were interrupted.

"What can I do to convince you to stay?"

Danni dropped the shredded marigold plant back into the tray and drew in her breath. "I don't know what to say."

"Say what you feel."

"As I recall, the fact that I said what I feel is what got us into this in the first place."

Sebastian squatted down beside her. "I know."

"I want more than you can give me. I want to go together to Wednesday night baseball games. I want to sit next to you in church every Sunday morning. I want to spend Sunday afternoons at the beach with our kids. I want you to wish on rainbows with me. I want you to believe in magic, because until you can do that, you can't believe in love. What do you want, Sebastian?"

His gaze met and held hers for long breathless moments. Finally, he said, "I don't want to lose you, Danielle, but I can't believe in magic."

"And therein lies the problem, doesn't it?"

Sebastian stood and stuffed his hands in his pockets. "I guess there's nothing left to say, is there?"

"There's a hell of a lot left to say. You just don't want to hear it."

"When do you leave?"

"Next Wednesday."

"Will I see you before—before you leave?"

"Probably not."

"Danni—"

"Sebastian," Danni broke in. "I'm tired of rehashing this. You can't be what I want, and I can't be what you want."

"I stuck to the rules," Sebastian muttered defensively as he turned to leave.

"*That's* your problem!" Danni threw down her gardening gloves and stalked into the house, slamming the door behind her.

Sebastian could've sworn he'd seen every animal within a three-hundred-mile radius of White Creek, but still he worked from morning till night. He barely had time for meals—not that he was hungry. So why did his days seem so long and why, as exhausted as he was, were his eyes red-rimmed from insomnia?

The reason was clear. It was her—that elusive

butterfly that had decided to try her wings and land just out of his reach. He wanted her back.

Fact: As much as he tried to convince himself otherwise, Danielle really wasn't a thing like Sharon. Sharon had flitted from one thing to another because she was never happy with anything. Danni had flitted only until she found what she wanted to do, and she'd stuck with it. He'd seen the hard work and dedication she'd devoted to her studies—and to her work with him. But would she be as true with her love? She'd have to be. As wildly passionate as she was, she'd held on to her virginity for twenty-five years. And then she'd given it to him . . . because she loved him.

So why was he still stuck in the rut of his past?

Fact: He was stuck because Danni was right. He was terrified. Terrified to leave it.

Fact: She was a butterfly. So? She wasn't one about the things that mattered. Besides, butterflies made life interesting.

Fact: She turned him on more than any other woman he'd ever met. Wasn't that worth hanging on to?

Fact: She believed in magic, and he didn't. So? He wasn't too old to learn how.

Sebastian nodded in satisfaction. Reasoning and logic won out every time.

"So what do I do next?" he said out loud, and Merlin jumped from the windowsill to the bed. He sat next to Sebastian and meowed once.

"You're right. If I go barreling over there right now and ask her to marry me, she'll never buy it. She'll think I'm doing it out of—guilt, or something. I'll have to approach it more subtly than that." He stared into the cat's odd-colored eyes for a long moment, then snapped his fingers. "Now that's an idea." He grabbed the telephone. Now to put his idea into action.

When Danni arrived home from her last exam, she opened the door to find her living room full of pink and purple balloons. In the midst of all the aerial clutter sat a fat white cardboard box with a pink bow on top.

Danni absently dropped her book bag in the chair and made a beeline for the box. When she lifted the lid, she caught her breath. There, nestled on a mound of pink tissue paper, sat a tiny porcelain Santa. Her fingers trembled as she opened the card tucked inside the box. All it said was, "You needed this for your collection."

There was no signature, but there didn't need to be. She'd known whom it was from even before she opened the box. What was this? Salve for a guilty conscience? She ought to go right over there and hand the figurine back, saying that at least he owed her the satisfaction of knowing that he was eaten up with guilt. Instead, she wiped away the tears, blew her nose, and set the figurine on her shelf, next to the Easter Bunny.

She waited until she saw Sebastian drive past in his truck before dashing down to his house and tacking a thank-you note on his front door. Yes, it was the coward's way out, but she really didn't think she could handle seeing him right now.

After eating dinner—or picking at her dinner—she halfheartedly began her packing. After all, she left day after tomorrow, as soon as she was sure she'd passed all her exams. Her grandma had left with the weak excuse that she was going to visit Magda. Danni figured she'd probably gone to see Lute Simpson.

About eight o'clock there was a knock at the front door. When she went to open it, no one was there except Merlin, looking extremely uncomfortable in a bright purple bow with a note attached. Danni rescued the cat from the ribbon and read the note. *Please, Danielle, I need to see you. Can you come now? Please send answer by return cat.*

Return cat? This wasn't at all like the Sebastian she knew. Bemused, she found herself writing *yes* on the note. As if he knew what to do next, the cat immediately trotted off down the street. Danni went back inside long enough to brush her hair, but she ignored the urge to change her clothes into something a little fancier than jeans and T-shirt. He'd seen her in jeans and T-shirt plenty of times.

When she arrived at Sebastian's ten minutes later, the house seemed dark except for low, flickering lights. Candles? There was a note on the front door. "Take off your shoes and enter." She slipped off her sandals, opened the door, and stepped inside. She was right. The room was lit only with candles. She felt something cool and silky beneath her feet and looked down. Pink rose petals.

A dainty glass jar sat on the table by a flickering pink candle. There was another note attached. *This is silver moondust. If you want to see me, take a handful, turn around three times, and toss it into the air, then close your eyes.*

Danni lifted the lid and looked inside the jar. It was filled with silver glitter. What in the world was he up to? She glanced around but didn't see either him or the cat anywhere, so she did as the note said. When she opened her eyes again, Sebastian stood in front of her. But it was a different Sebastian than she'd ever seen. He was dressed all in blue—blue socks, blue tennis shoes, blue jeans, and an electric-blue sweatshirt.

"I—uh—thought you didn't wear much blue," she finally said after several moments of silence.

"Magda said it's my color. I thought I'd keep an open mind."

"An open mind?"

"I'm going to try to keep an open mind about a lot of things."

"Even six-toed cats with odd eyes?" Danni said with a ghost of a smile.

"Especially them. And beautiful vets who believe in magic." He reached out a finger and caught a teardrop that suddenly spilled over and ran down her cheek. "I believe in extraordinary cats, Santa Claus, and you. I hope you can believe in me too."

"Believe what?" she whispered.

"Believe that I love you."

Danni drew in a shaky breath and took a step back. "Why should I believe you now when you didn't love me a couple of days ago?"

"I loved you then. I just—I was afraid. You were right, Danni. It seemed safer to stay in my little rut than to take a chance on getting ground into the dirt again."

"What made you decide to take the chance now?"

"I started thinking about what my life was going to be like with you gone." He took both of her hands in his and pulled her over to sit on the sofa. "I can't eat right. I can't seem to sleep without you in my arms."

"You never actually slept with me in your arms. You kicked me out, as I recall."

"I know. My mistake. If I had the chance to do it over, I'd never let you out of my arms all night or out of my sight during the day. My days are all long, dull, and impossibly lonely without you."

Danni tugged one of her hands from his long enough to brush away another tear, then another. "What about the Wednesday night baseball games together and the Sunday mornings in church together?"

"Even the Sunday afternoons at the beach with our kids."

"What about wishing on rainbows?" Danni smiled a little.

Sebastian shrugged. "I'll keep an open mind. After all, if you can love an old stuck-in-a-rut like me, then the world is full of all kinds of possibilities."

"That's what I've been trying to tell you."

"So I'm a slow learner, but once I've learned, I know it by heart. You could teach me to believe in magic, Danielle," he said tenderly. "But it might take a lifetime to do it."

"Then we'd better get started." She moved into his arms and clung with all her strength.

He kissed her then, a long, slow, almost unbearably sweet kiss full of promises—and commitments. "I missed you," he murmured against her lips. "You're not getting away from me again. As a matter of fact," he said as he gathered her up into his arms and headed upstairs, "I may not even let you out of bed again."

"I don't exactly plan on fighting to get out of your bed."

"Our bed."

Even though their passion burned hot, their loving was long and slow, because they knew they had a lifetime. They both gave and took with equal intensity until it was no longer possible to distinguish whose sighs and moans of pleasure were whose. When they finally reached the top of the mountain, they tumbled into space together.

The sun reached long golden fingers across the bed when Sebastian awoke. He smiled. Best night's sleep he'd had in a week—when he'd finally gotten to sleep, that is. He hooked his arms more securely around Danni. This was the reason for his good night's sleep. After all, there was something infinitely satisfying about sleeping with the woman you love in your arms, especially when the sleep came after the kind of loving that went before.

The telephone jangled, and he scrambled for it, wanting to let Danni sleep a little longer. He hadn't given her much rest last night. He smiled again at the memory as he picked up the receiver. "Hello?"

"Do you have my granddaughter over there?"

Was she going to march down here with a shotgun? He hoped so. "Uh, as a matter of fact, I do."

"That's okay, then. I just wanted to know where she was." With a cheery good-bye Virgie hung up.

"Gran?" Danni murmured sleepily.

"Gran."

She levered herself up on one elbow, pushing away a swathe of hair that fell over her face. She looked at Sebastian intently.

"What?"

"I'm making sure it's you, that's all. And that it's real."

"It's real, all right. What else would it be?"

She smiled. "A dream. Magic."

"No dream. Reality is better."

"Infinitely. And here is someone who agrees," she said as Merlin jumped up on the foot of the bed. "Uh-oh. He's got another mouse."

Sebastian sat up and pointed an imperious

finger at the door. “Not in here, you don’t, you reprobate.”

The cat immediately jumped off the bed and walked just outside the door of the room. He let the mouse go and watched it scamper off, then jumped back up on the bed and settled down to take a nap.

Danni cast a cautious glance at Sebastian. “He, um, is a very bright cat.”

“That’s not it, and you know it, Danni. It’s magic. Pure and simple. The same magic that brought you into my life.”

He pulled her back into his arms and pressed her down into the mattress. Magic, indeed!

EPILOGUE

"Where do you want to go for our second honeymoon?" Sebastian asked his wife, as he spread travel brochures all over the bed.

Danni stretched and sat up. "What do you mean, 'second honeymoon'?" She smiled and kissed her husband good morning. "We've already had a second and a third and a fourth. This would be our fifth."

He gave her another kiss. "Actually, our life has been one long honeymoon, so this is a continuation." He ran a hand over Danni's breasts. "So where do you want to continue it this summer?"

Danni arched her back under her husband's caresses. "Can't we just stay here?"

"What? Why? We've only seen the Eiffel Tower, the canals of Venice, the Black Forest, and the Alps. There's a whole big world out there, and the whole month of July to see it in. Grant Richards will cover for me, like always."

"I think there are other things we ought to spend that money on."

"Like what? We save up the whole year for this."

Danni paused, then said, "Like a cradle."

"A cradle?" There was a long moment of silence, then, barely whispered, "A cradle?" He immediately slid his hand from his wife's breasts to her still-flat abdomen. "A cradle. I thought the doctor said—"

"That I couldn't get pregnant? He did. And when I saw him this afternoon, he said the same thing right before the blood test came back positive."

Sebastian could feel his throat swelling tight with emotion. "This is why you haven't been eating breakfast recently, and why you've been taking naps every afternoon."

Danni reached up and wiped a tear from her husband's cheek. "It goes with the territory."

"A baby. Our baby."

"It's magic."

"Oh, no, sweetheart. It's way past magic. It's a bona fide miracle."

Danni looped her arms around Sebastian's neck and moved suggestively against him. "The doctor said I should get plenty of exercise."

"We certainly must follow the doctor's orders," he murmured against her throat as he nibbled a trail down to her breasts.

"I love you, Dr. Kent."

"And I love you, Dr. Kent."

Merlin sat in his customary place on the windowsill and watched the silly antics of the humans on the bed. They indulged in these ridiculous activities quite often. But cats were above that sort of nonsense. He yawned and closed his eyes.

THE EDITOR'S CORNER

Celebrate the most romantic month of the year with LOVESWEPT! In the six fabulous novels coming your way, you'll thrill to the sexiest heroes and cheer for the most spirited heroines as they discover the power of passion. It's all guaranteed to get you in the mood for love.

Starting the lineup is the ever-popular Fayrene Preston with **STORM SONG**, LOVESWEPT #666—and Noah McKane certainly comes across like a force of nature. He's the hottest act in town, but he never gives interviews, never lets anyone get close to him—until Cate Gallin persuades the powerfully sensual singer to let her capture him on film. Nobody knows the secret they share, the bonds of pain and emotion that go soul-deep . . . or the risks they're taking when Cate accepts the challenge to reveal his stunning talent—without hurting the only man she's ever loved. This compelling novel is proof positive of why Fayrene is one of the best-loved authors of the genre.

SLIGHTLY SHADY by Jan Hudson, LOVESWEPT #667, is Maggie Marino's first impression of the brooding desperado she sees in the run-down bar. On the run from powerful forces, she's gotten stranded deep in the heart of Texas, and the last thing she wants is to tangle with a mesmerizing outlaw who calls himself Shade. But Shade knows just how to comfort a woman, and Maggie soon finds herself surrendering to his sizzling looks—even as she wonders what secret he's hiding. To tantalize you even further, we'll tell you that Shade is truly Paul Berringer, a tiger of the business world and brother of the Berringer twins who captivated you in **BIG AND BRIGHT** and **CALL ME SIN**. So don't miss out on Paul's own story. Bad boys don't come any better, and as usual Jan Hudson's writing shines with humor and sizzles with sensuality.

Please give a warm welcome to Gayle Kasper and her very first LOVESWEPT, **TENDER, LOVING CURE**, #668. As you may have guessed, this utterly delightful romance features a doctor, and there isn't a finer one than Joel Benedict. He'd do anything to become even better—except attend a sex talk seminar. He changes his mind, though, when he catches a glimpse of the teacher. Maggie Springer is a temptress who makes Joel think of private lessons, and when a taste of her kissable lips sparks the fire beneath his cool facade, he starts to believe that it's possible for him to love once more. We're happy to be Gayle's publisher, and this terrific novel will show you why.

Sally Goldenbaum returns to LOVESWEPT with **MOONLIGHT ON MONTEREY BAY**, #669. The beach in that part of California has always been special to Sam Eastland, and when he goes to his empty house there, he doesn't expect to discover a beautiful nymph. Interior decorator Maddie Ames fights to convince him that only she can create a sanctuary to soothe his troubled spirit . . . and he's too spellbound to refuse. But when their attraction flares into burning passion and Sam fears he can't give Maddie the joy she deserves, she must persuade him not to underestimate the power of love. Vibrant with heartfelt emotion, this romance showcases Sally's evocative writing. Welcome back, Sally!

A spooky manor house, things that go bump in the night—all this and more await you in **MIDNIGHT LADY**, LOVESWEPT #670, by Linda Wisdom. The granddaughter of the king of horror movies, Samantha Lyons knows all about scare tactics, and she uses them to try to keep Kyle Fletcher from getting the inside scoop about her family's film studio. But the devastatingly handsome reporter isn't about to abandon the story—or break the sensual magic that has woven itself around him and beautiful Sam . . . even if wooing her means facing down ghosts! Hold on to your seats because Linda is about to take you on a roller-coaster ride of dangerous desires and exquisite sensations.

It **LOOKS LIKE LOVE** when Drew Webster first sees Jill Stuart in Susan Connell's new LOVESWEPT, #671. Jill is a delicious early-morning surprise, clad in silky lingerie, kneeling in Drew's uncle's yard, and coaxing a puppy into her arms. Drew knows instantly that she wouldn't have to beg him to come running, and he sets off on a passionate courtship. To Jill, temptation has never looked or felt so good, but when Drew insists that there's a thief in the retirement community she manages, she tells him it can't be true, that she has everything under control. Drew wants to trust her, but can he believe the angel who's stolen his heart?

Susan delivers a wonderful love story that will warm your heart.

Happy reading!

With warmest wishes,

Nita Taublib

Nita Taublib

Associate Publisher

P.S. Don't miss the exciting women's novels from Bantam that are coming your way in February—**THE BELOVED SCOUNDREL** by nationally bestselling author Iris Johansen, a tempestuous tale of abduction, seduction, and surrender that sweeps from the shimmering halls of Regency England to the decadent haunts of a notorious rogue; **VIXEN** by award-winning author Jane Feather, a spectacular historical romance in which an iron-willed nobleman suddenly becomes the guardian of a mischievous, orphaned beauty; and **ONE FINE DAY** by supertalented Theresa Weir, which tells the searing story of a second chance for happiness for Molly and Austin Bennet, two memorable characters from Theresa's previous novel **FOREVER**. We'll be giving you a sneak peek at these terrific books in next month's LOVESWEPTs. And immediately following this page look for a preview of the exciting romances from Bantam that are *available now!*

Don't miss these exciting books by your favorite Bantam authors

On sale in December:

DESIRE

by Amanda Quick

LONG TIME COMING

by Sandra Brown

STRANGER IN MY ARMS

by R.J. Kaiser

WHERE DOLPHINS GO

by Peggy Webb

And in hardcover from Doubleday

AMAZON LILY

by Theresa Weir

"One of the hottest and most prolific writers in romance today . . .
Her heroines are always spunky women you'd love to know, and her heroes are dashing guys you'd love to love."
—*USA Today*

Amanda Quick

New York Times bestselling author of
DANGEROUS and **DECEPTION**

DESIRE

This spectacular novel is Amanda Quick's first medieval romance!

From the windswept, craggy coast of a remote British isle comes the thrilling tale of a daring lady and a dangerous knight who are bound by the tempests of fate and by the dawning of desire . . .

"There was something you wished to discuss with me, sir?"

"Aye. Our marriage."

Clare flinched, but she did not fall off the bench. Under the circumstances, she considered that a great accomplishment. "You are very direct about matters, sir."

He looked mildly surprised. "I see no point in being otherwise."

"Nor do I. Very well, sir, let me be blunt. In spite of your efforts to establish yourself in everyone's eyes as the sole suitor for my hand, I must tell you again that your expectations are unrealistic."

"Nay, madam," Gareth said very quietly. "'Tis your expectations that are unrealistic. I read the letter you sent to Lord Thurston. It is obvious you hope to marry a phantom, a man who does not exist. I fear you must settle for something less than perfection."

She lifted her chin. "You think that no man can be found who suits my requirements?"

"I believe that we are both old enough and wise enough to know that marriage is a practical matter. It has nothing to do with the passions that the troubadours make so much of in their foolish ballads."

Clare clasped her hands together very tightly. "Kindly do not condescend to lecture me on the subject of marriage, sir. I am only too well aware that in my case it is a matter of duty, not desire. But in truth, when I composed my recipe for a husband, I did not believe that I was asking for so very much."

"Mayhap you will discover enough good points in me to satisfy you, madam."

Clare blinked. "Do you actually believe that?"

"I would ask you to examine closely what I have to offer. I think that I can meet a goodly portion of your requirements."

She surveyed him from head to toe. "You most definitely do not meet my requirements in the matter of size."

"Concerning my size, as I said earlier, there is little I can do about it, but I assure you I do not generally rely upon it to obtain my ends."

Clare gave a ladylike snort of disbelief.

" 'Tis true. I prefer to use my wits rather than muscle whenever possible."

"Sir, I shall be frank. I want a man of peace for this isle. Desire has never known violence. I intend to keep things that way. I do not want a husband who thrives on the sport of war."

He looked down at her with an expression of surprise. "I have no love of violence or war."

Clare raised her brows. "Are you going to tell me that you have no interest in either? You, who carry a sword with a terrible name? You, who wear a reputation as a destroyer of murderers and thieves?"

"I did not say I had no interest in such matters. I have, after all, used a warrior's skills to make my way in the world. They are the tools of my trade, that's all."

"A fine point, sir."

"But a valid one. I have grown weary of violence, madam. I seek a quiet, peaceful life."

Clare did not bother to hide her skepticism. "An interesting statement, given your choice of career."

"I did not have much choice in the matter of my career," Gareth said. "Did you?"

"Nay, but that is—"

"Let us go on to your second requirement. You wrote that you desire a man of cheerful countenance and even temperament."

She stared at him, astonished. "You consider yourself a man of cheerful countenance?"

"Nay, I admit that I have been told my countenance is somewhat less than cheerful. But I am most definitely a man of even temperament."

"I do not believe that for a moment, sir."

"I promise you, it is the truth. You may inquire of anyone who knows me. Ask Sir Ulrich. He has been my companion for years. He will tell you that I am the most even-tempered of men. I am not given to fits of rage or foul temper."

Or to mirth and laughter, either, Clare thought as she met his smoky crystal eyes. "Very well, I shall grant that you may be even-tempered in a certain sense, although that was not quite what I had in mind."

"You see? We are making progress here." Gareth reached up to grasp a limb of the apple tree. "Now, then, to continue. Regarding your last requirement, I remind you yet again that I can read."

Clare cast about frantically for a fresh tactic. "Enough, sir. I grant that you meet a small number of my requirements if one interprets them very broadly. But what about our own? Surely there are some specific things you seek in a wife."

"My requirements?" Gareth looked taken back by the question. "My requirements in a wife are simple, madam. I believe that you will satisfy them."

"Because I hold lands and the recipes of a plump perfume business? Think twice before you decide that is sufficient to satisfy you sir. We live a simple life here on Desire. Quite boring in most respects. You are a man who is no doubt accustomed to the grand entertainments provided in the households of great lords."

"I can do without such entertainments, my lady. They hold no appeal for me."

"You have obviously lived an adventurous, exciting life," Clare persisted. "Will you find contentment in the business of growing flowers and making perfumes?"

"Aye, madam, I will," Gareth said with soft satisfaction.

"'Tis hardly a career suited to a knight of your reputation, sir."

"Rest assured that here on Desire I expect to find the things that are most important to me."

Clare lost patience with his reasonableness. "And just what are those things, sir?"

"Lands, a hall of my own, and a woman who can give me a family." Gareth reached down and pulled her to her feet as effortlessly as though she were fashioned of thistledown. "You can provide me with all of those things, lady. That makes you very valuable to me. Do not imagine that I will not protect you well. And do not think that I will let you slip out of my grasp."

"But—"

Gareth brought his mouth down on hers, silencing her protest.

LONG TIME COMING

by

SANDRA BROWN

Blockbuster author Sandra Brown—whose name is almost synonymous with the *New York Times* bestseller list—offers up a classic romantic novel that aches with emotion and sizzles with passion . . .

For sixteen years Marnie Hibbs had raised her sister's son as her own, hoping that her love would make up for the father David would never know . . . dreaming that someday David's father would find his way back into her life. And then one afternoon Marnie looked up and Law Kincaid was there, as strong and heartbreakingly handsome as ever. Flooded with bittersweet memories, Marnie yearned to lose herself in his arms, yet a desperate fear held her back, for this glorious man who had given her David now had the power to take him away. . . .

The Porsche crept along the street like a sleek black panther. Hugging the curb, its engine purred so deep and low it sounded like a predator's growl.

Marnie Hibbs was kneeling in the fertile soil of her flower bed, digging among the impatiens under the ligustrum bushes and cursing the little bugs that made three meals a day of them, when the sound of the car's motor attracted her attention. She glanced at it over her shoulder, then panicked as it came to a stop in front of her house.

"Lord, is it that late?" she muttered. Dropping her trowel, she stood up and brushed the clinging damp earth off her bare knees.

She reached up to push her dark bangs off her forehead before she realized that she still had on her heavy gardening gloves. Quickly she peeled them off and dropped them beside the trowel, all the while watching the driver get out of the sports car and start up her front walk.

Glancing at her wristwatch, she saw that she hadn't lost track of time. He was just very early for their appointment, and as a result, she wasn't going to make a very good first impression. Being hot, sweaty, and dirty was no way to meet a client. And she needed this commission badly.

Forcing a smile, she moved down the sidewalk to greet him, nervously trying to remember if she had left the house and studio reasonably neat when she decided to do an hour's worth of yard work. She had planned to tidy up before he arrived.

She might look like the devil, but she didn't want to appear intimidated. Self-confident friendliness was the only way to combat the disadvantage of having been caught looking her worst.

He was still several yards away from her when she greeted him. "Hello," she said with a bright smile. "Obviously we got our signals switched. I thought you weren't coming until later."

"I decided this diabolical game of yours had gone on long enough."

Marnie's sneakers skidded on the old concrete walk as she came to an abrupt halt. She tilted her head in stunned surprise. "I'm sorry, I—"

"Who the hell are you, lady?"

"Miss Hibbs. Who do you think?"

"Never heard of you. Just what the devil are you up to?"

"Up to?" She glanced around helplessly, as though the giant sycamores in her front yard might provide an answer to this bizarre interrogation.

"Why've you been sending me those letters?"

"Letters?"

He was clearly furious, and her lack of comprehension only seemed to make him angrier. He bore down on her like a hawk on a field mouse, until she had to bow her back to look up at him. The summer sun was behind him, casting him in silhouette.

He was blond, tall, trim, and dressed in casual slacks and a sport shirt—all stylish, impeccably so. He was wearing opaque aviator glasses, so she couldn't see his eyes, but if they were as belligerent as his expression and stance, she was better off not seeing them.

"I don't know what you're talking about."

"The letters, lady, the letters." He strained the words through a set of strong white teeth.

"*What* letters?"

"Don't play dumb."

"Are you sure you've got the right house?"

He took another step forward. "I've got the right house," he said in a voice that was little more than a snarl.

"Obviously you don't." She didn't like being put on the defensive, especially by someone she'd never met over something of which she was totally ignorant. "You're either crazy or drunk, but in any case, you're *wrong*. I'm not the person you're looking for and I demand that you leave my property. Now."

"You were expecting me. I could tell by the way you spoke to me."

"I thought you were the man from the advertising agency."

"Well, I'm not."

"Thank God." She would hate having to do business with someone this irrational and ill-tempered.

"You know damn well who I am," he said, peeling off the sunglasses.

Marnie sucked in a quick, sharp breath and fell back a step because she did indeed know who he was. She raised a hand to her chest in an attempt at keeping her jumping heart in place. "Law," she gasped.

"That's right. Law Kincaid. Just like you wrote it on the envelopes."

She was shocked to see him after all these years, standing only inches in front of her. This time he wasn't merely a familiar image in the newspaper or on her television screen. He was flesh and blood. The years had been kind to that flesh, improving his looks, not eroding them.

She wanted to stand and stare, but he was staring at her with unmitigated contempt and no recognition at all. "Let's go inside, Mr. Kincaid," she suggested softly.

STRANGER IN MY ARMS

by

R.J. KAISER

With the chilling tension of Hitchcock and the passionate heat of Sandra Brown, STRANGER IN MY ARMS is a riveting novel of romantic suspense in which a woman with amnesia suspects she is a target for murder.

Here is a look at this powerful novel . . .

"Tell me who you are, Carter, where you came from, about your past—everything."

He complied, giving me a modest summary of his life. He'd started his career in New York and formed a partnership with a British firm in London. When his partners suffered financial difficulties, he convinced my father to buy them out. Altogether he'd been in Europe for twelve years.

Carter was forty, ten years older than I. He'd been born and raised in Virginia, where his parents still resided. He'd attended Dartmouth and the Harvard Business School. In addition to the villa he had a house in Kensington, a flat off the avenue Bosquet in Paris, and a small farm outside Charlottesville, Virginia.

After completing his discourse, he leaned back and sipped his coffee. I watched him while Yvonne cleared the table.

Carter Bass was an attractive man with sophistication and class. He was well-spoken, educated. But mainly he appealed to me because I felt a connection with him, tortured though it was. We'd been dancing around each other since he'd appeared on the scene, our history at war with our more immediate and intangible feelings toward each other.

I could only assume that the allure he held for me had to do with the fact that he was both a stranger and my husband. My body, in effect, remembered Carter as my mind could not.

I picked up my coffee cup, but paused with it at my lips. Something had been troubling me for some time and I decided to blurt it out. "Do you have a mistress, Carter?"

He blinked. "What kind of a question is that?"

"A serious one. You know all about me, it's only fair I know about you."

"I don't have a mistress."

"Are you lonely?"

He smiled indulgently. "Hillary, we have an unspoken agreement. You don't ask and neither do I."

"Then you don't want to talk about it? I should mind my own business, is that what you mean?"

He contemplated me. "Maybe we should step out onto the terrace for some air—sort of clear our mental palate."

"If you like."

Carter came round and helped me up. "Could I interest you in a brandy?"

"I don't think so. I enjoyed the wine. That's really all I'd like."

He took my arm and we went through the salon and onto the terrace. He kept his hand on my elbow, though I was no longer shaky. His attention was flattering, and I decided I liked the changing chemistry between us, even though I had so many doubts.

It was a clear night and there were countless stars. I inhaled the pleasantly cool air and looked at my husband. Carter let his hand drop away.

"I miss this place," he said.

"Did I drive you away?"

"No, I've stayed away by choice."

"It's all so sad," I said, staring off down the dark valley. "I think we're a tragic pair. People shouldn't be as unhappy as we seem to be."

"You're talking about the past. Amnesiacs aren't supposed to do that, my dear."

I smiled at his teasing.

"I'm learning all about myself, about us, very quickly."

"I wonder if you're better off not knowing," he said, a trace of sadness in his voice.

"I can't run away from who I am," I replied.

"No, I suppose you can't."

"You'd like for me to change, though, wouldn't you?"

"What difference does it make? Your condition is temporary. It's probably better in the long run to treat you as the person I know you to be."

His words seemed cruel—or at least unkind—though what he was saying was not only obvious, it was also reasonable. Why should he assume the burden of my sins? I sighed and looked away.

"I'd like to believe in you, Hillary," he said. "But it isn't as simple as just giving you the benefit of the doubt."

"If I could erase the past, I would." My eyes shimmered. "But even if you were willing, *they* wouldn't let me."

Carter knew whom I was referring to. "They" were the police, and "they" were coming for me in the morning, though their purpose was still somewhat vague. "They" were the whole issue, it seemed to me—maybe the final arbiter of who I really was. My past not only defined me, it was my destiny.

"I don't think you should jump to any conclusions," he said. "Let's wait and see what they have to say."

He reached out and took my bare arms, seemingly to savor the feel of my skin. His hands were quite warm, and he gripped me firmly as he searched my eyes. I was sure then that he had brought me to the terrace to touch me, to connect with me physically. He had wanted to be close to me. And maybe I'd come along because I wanted to be close to him.

There were signs of desire in Carter's eyes. Heat. My heart picked up its beat when he lowered his mouth toward mine. His kiss was tender and it aroused me. I'd hungered for this—for the affirmation, for the affection—more than I knew. But still I wasn't prepared for it. I didn't expect to want him as much as I did.

I kissed Carter every bit as deeply as he kissed me. Then, at exactly the same moment, we pulled apart, retreating as swiftly as we'd come together. When I looked into his eyes I saw the reflection of my own feelings—the same doubt, distrust, and fear that I myself felt.

And when he released me, I realized that the issues separating us remained unresolved. The past, like the future, was undeniable. The morning would come. It would come much too soon.

WHERE DOLPHINS GO

by

PEGGY WEBB

"Ms. Webb has an inventive mind brimming with originality that makes all of her books special reading."
—*Romantic Times*

To Susan Riley, the dolphins at the Oceanfront Research Center were her last chance to reach her frail, broken child. Yet when she brought Jeffy to the Center, she never expected to have to contend with a prickly doctor who made it clear that he didn't intend to get involved. Quiet, handsome, and hostile, Paul Taylor was a wounded man, and when Susan learned of the tragedy behind his anguish, she knew she had to help. But what began as compassion soon turned to desire, and now Susan was falling for a man who belonged to someone else. . . .

"A woman came to see me today," Bill said. "A woman and a little boy."

Paul went very still.

"Her name is Susan . . . Susan Riley. She knew about the center from that article in the newspaper last week."

There had been many articles written about Dr. Bill McKenzie and the research he did with dolphins. The most recent one, though, had delved into the personality of the dolphins themselves. An enterprising reporter had done his homework. "Dolphins," he had written, "relate well to people. Some even seem to have extrasensory perception. They seem to sense when a person is sick or hurt or depressed."

"Her little boy has a condition called truncus arteriosus . . ." Bill squinted in the way he always did when he was judging a person's reaction.

Paul was careful not to show one. *Truncus arteriosus. A condition of the heart. Malfunctioning arteries. Surgery required.*

"Bill, I don't practice medicine anymore."

"I'm not asking you to practice medicine. I'm asking you to listen."

"I'm listening."

"The boy was scheduled for surgery, but he had a stroke before it could be performed."

For God's sake, Paul. Do something. DO SOMETHING!

"Bill . . ."

"The child is depressed, doesn't respond to anything, anybody. She thought the dolphins might be the answer. She wanted to bring him here on a regular basis."

"You told her no, of course."

"I'm a marine biologist, not a psychologist." Bill slumped in his chair. "I told her no."

"The child needs therapy, not dolphins."

"That's what I thought, but now . . ." Bill gave Paul that squinty-eyed look. "You're a doctor, Paul. Maybe if I let her bring the boy here during feeding times—"

"No. Dammit, Bill. Look at me. I can't even help myself, let alone a dying child and a desperate mother."

Bill looked down at his shoes and counted to ten under his breath. When he looked up Paul could see the pity in his eyes.

He hated that most of all. . . .

Susan hadn't meant to cry.

She knew before she came to the Oceanfront Research Center that her chances of success were slim. And yet she had to try. She couldn't live with herself if she didn't do everything in her power to help Jeffy.

Her face was already wet with tears as she lifted her child from his stroller and placed him in the car. He was so lifeless, almost as if he had already died and had forgotten to take his body with him. When she bent over him to fasten the seat belt, her tears dripped onto his still face.

He didn't even notice.

She swiped at her tears, mad at herself. Crying wasn't going to help Jeffy. Crying wasn't going to help either of them.

Resolutely she folded the stroller and put it in the backseat. Then she blew her nose and climbed into the driver's seat. Couldn't let Jeffy know she was sad. Did he see? Did he know?

The doctors had assured her that he did. That the stroke damage had been confined to areas of the brain that affected his motor control. That his bright little mind and his personality were untouched. And yet, he sat beside her like some discarded rag doll, staring at nothing.

Fighting hard against the helpless feeling she sometimes got when she looked at Jeffy, she turned the key in the ignition and waited for the old engine to warm up. She was not helpless. And she refused to let herself become that way.

"Remember that little song you love so much, Jeffy? The one Mommy wrote?" Jeffy stared at his small sneakers.

Sweat plastered Susan's hair to the sides of her face and made the back of her sundress stick to the seat.

"Mommy's going to sing it to you, darling, while we drive." She put the car into gear and backed out of the parking space, giving herself time to get the quiver out of her voice. She was *not* going to cry again. "You remember the words, don't you, sweetheart? Help Mommy sing, Jeffy."

" 'Sing with a voice of gladness; sing with a voice of joy.'" Susan's voice was neither glad nor joyful, but at least it no longer quivered. Control was easier in the daytime. It was at night, lying in the dark all by herself, when she lost it. She had cried herself to sleep many nights, muffling the sounds in the pillow in case Jeffy, sleeping in the next room, could hear.

" 'Shout for the times of goodness.' " How many good times could Jeffy remember? " 'Shout for the time of cheer.' " How many happy times had he had? Born with a heart condition, he had missed the ordinary joys other children took for granted—chasing a dog, kicking a ball, tumbling in the leaves, outrunning the wind.

" 'Sing with a voice that's hopeful . . . ' " Susan sang on, determined to be brave, determined to bring her child back from that dark, silent world he had entered.

As the car took a curve, Jeffy's head lolled to the side so he was staring straight at her. All the brightness of childhood that should be in his eyes was dulled over by four years of pain and defeat.

Why do you let me hurt?

The message in those eyes made her heart break.

The song died on her lips, the last clear notes lingering in the car like a party guest who didn't know it was time to go home. Susan turned her head to look out the window.

Biloxi was parching under the late afternoon sun. Dust devils shimmered in the streets. Palm trees, sagging and dusty, looked as tired as she felt. It seemed years since she had had a peaceful night's sleep. An eternity since she had had a day of fun and relaxation.

She was selfish to the core. Thinking about her own needs, her own desires. She had to think about Jeffy. There must be something that would spark his interest besides the dolphins.

And don't miss these heart-stopping romances from Bantam Books, on sale in January

THE BELOVED SCOUNDREL
by the nationally bestselling author
Iris Johansen
"You'll be riveted from beginning to end as [Iris Johansen] holds you captive to a love story of grand proportions."
—*Romantic Times* on
The Magnificent Rogue

VIXEN
by **Jane Feather**
A passionate tale of an iron-willed nobleman who suddenly becomes the guardian of a mischievous, orphaned beauty.

ONE FINE DAY
by **Theresa Weir**
"Theresa Weir's writing is poignant, passionate and powerful. *One Fine Day* delivers intense emotion and compelling characters that will capture the hearts of readers."
—*New York Times* bestselling
author Jayne Ann Krentz

OFFICIAL RULES

To enter the sweepstakes below carefully follow all instructions found elsewhere in this offer.

The **Winners Classic** will award prizes with the following approximate maximum values: 1 Grand Prize: $26,500 (or $25,000 cash alternate); 1 First Prize: $3,000; 5 Second Prizes: $400 each; 35 Third Prizes: $100 each; 1,000 Fourth Prizes: $7.50 each. Total maximum retail value of Winners Classic Sweepstakes is $42,500. Some presentations of this sweepstakes may contain individual entry numbers corresponding to one or more of the aforementioned prize levels. To determine the Winners, individual entry numbers will first be compared with the winning numbers preselected by computer. For winning numbers not returned, prizes will be awarded in random drawings from among all eligible entries received. Prize choices may be offered at various levels. If a winner chooses an automobile prize, all license and registration fees, taxes, destination charges and, other expenses not offered herein are the responsibility of the winner. If a winner chooses a trip, travel must be complete within one year from the time the prize is awarded. Minors must be accompanied by an adult. Travel companion(s) must also sign release of liability. Trips are subject to space and departure availability. Certain black-out dates may apply.

The following applies to the sweepstakes named above:

No purchase necessary. You can also enter the sweepstakes by sending your name and address to: P.O. Box 508, Gibbstown, N.J. 08027. Mail each entry separately. Sweepstakes begins 6/1/93. Entries must be received by 12/30/94. Not responsible for lost, late, damaged, misdirected, illegible or postage due mail. Mechanically reproduced entries are not eligible. All entries become property of the sponsor and will not be returned.

Prize Selection/Validations: Selection of winners will be conducted no later than 5:00 PM on January 28, 1995, by an independent judging organization whose decisions are final. Random drawings will be held at 1211 Avenue of the Americas, New York, N.Y. 10036. Entrants need not be present to win. Odds of winning are determined by total number of entries received. Circulation of this sweepstakes is estimated not to exceed 200 million. All prizes are guaranteed to be awarded and delivered to winners. Winners will be notified by mail and may be required to complete an affidavit of eligibility and release of liability which must be returned within 14 days of date on notification or alternate winners will be selected in a random drawing. Any prize notification letter or any prize returned to a participating sponsor, Bantam Doubleday Dell Publishing Group, Inc., its participating divisions or subsidiaries, or the independent judging organization as undeliverable will be awarded to an alternate winner. Prizes are not transferable. No substitution for prizes except as offered or as may be necessary due to unavailability, in which case a prize of equal or greater value will be awarded. Prizes will be awarded approximately 90 days after the drawing. All taxes are the sole responsibility of the winners. Entry constitutes permission (except where prohibited by law) to use winners' names, hometowns, and likenesses for publicity purposes without further or other compensation. Prizes won by minors will be awarded in the name of parent or legal guardian.

Participation: Sweepstakes open to residents of the United States and Canada, except for the province of Quebec. Sweepstakes sponsored by Bantam Doubleday Dell Publishing Group, Inc., (BDD), 1540 Broadway, New York, NY 10036. Versions of this sweepstakes with different graphics and prize choices will be offered in conjunction with various solicitations or promotions by different subsidiaries and divisions of BDD. Where applicable, winners will have their choice of any prize offered at level won. Employees of BDD, its divisions, subsidiaries, advertising agencies, independent judging organization, and their immediate family members are not eligible.

Canadian residents, in order to win, must first correctly answer a time limited arithmetical skill testing question. Void in Puerto Rico, Quebec and wherever prohibited or restricted by law. Subject to all federal, state, local and provincial laws and regulations. For a list of major prize winners (available after 1/29/95): send a self-addressed, stamped envelope entirely separate from your entry to: Sweepstakes Winners, P.O. Box 517, Gibbstown, NJ 08027. Requests must be received by 12/30/94. DO NOT SEND ANY OTHER CORRESPONDENCE TO THIS P.O. BOX.

SWP 7/93